Farther to Fall

J L Libstaff

Key Literary Concepts
Washington

For information, address Key Literary Concepts, P O Box 925
Vaughn WA 98394

Printed in the United States of America

First Edition: April 2008
2nd Printing July 2009
Second Edition November 2014

Libstaff, J L
Farther to Fall / Libstaff

Library of Congress Control Number 2014920641

ISBN 978-0-9816065-7-6

10 9 8 7 6 5 4 3 2 1

For Pamela, Heidi and Jim

Acknowledgments

Special thanks to my wife, Pam who has continued to encourage and support me throughout these many years and attempted to keep me honest. Susan Saxon Tao who inspired me to continue when I wanted to give up. Deanie, Irene, Carolyn and Watermark Writers for your input, suggestions, identifying notes and your insightful counsel.

Farther to Fall

When you think you've hit the bottom,
there is always

Farther to Fall

PROLOG

She stood waist deep in the water, sobbing, rocking back and forth, the body of a small child pressed tight against her chest. Hundreds of people lined the bank of the lake and watched, not one stirred to help. I gently pushed forward through the crowd and they parted without noticing my presence. I stepped into the icy water and waded fifteen feet to her side. Though waves pressed against my clothes, I felt neither cold nor wet.

The devastation had drawn her features into a Salvador Dali portrait of Hell. Tears poured from deep crevices that were her eyes and dripped from her chin to the lake like rain. From somewhere deep within, an ancient, almost imperceptible growl vibrated. I felt it before I heard the sound, as though her passion, her life were draining from her as she held the body of her child.

I touched her shoulder with my right hand. She didn't move. Still unaware of my presence, she suffered her pain alone. I pulled her close and hugged her, the lifeless boy between us.

Her eyes opened slightly and she raised her head to see me. I looked deep into her darkness with all the love and compassion I knew. Her eyes closed again as she lowered her head to the boy's shoulder. Her remaining strength seemed to dissolve.

She became as limp and frail as the boy and I held them both to prevent them slipping deeper into the water.

I slowly raised my left hand and placed it over the boy's face. She tensed, strength flowed through her and she looked at me with sudden terror. She tried to pull from my grasp but I held her with my arm and would not let her go.

Her eyes opened wide and she mouthed words that didn't come. Questions, fear, anguish, and then panic. She began to thrash and twist but I held tight. I moved my hand up, and brushed the wet, stringy hair from her boy's face. She calmed slightly as she watched. I bent forward and kissed her son on the forehead. His flesh was cold and rigid. She began to struggle again, pulling away and mouthed "No, No, No!!" repeatedly, though only silence came from her lips. I held them both in a hug and gently 'shushed' her as a parent would a frightened child. Suddenly the boy between us kicked his foot and jerked softly, though strong enough to catch her attention. She stiffened and looked down at him. He moved ever so slightly and she gazed back at me in shock. I smiled and nodded to her son. As she glanced back, the boy coughed and began to purge water from his lungs. A moment later he burst into a cry that echoed across the lake and filled the forest.

The woman stopped breathing and gaped at her boy as she watched him scream and writhe in her arms. As realization began to register, her own life surged back. She gasped and began to laugh as she squeezed him tight enough to nearly choke him. He screamed and fought her harder.

The crowd on the shore came to life. Their combined voices began softly, as the hum of an electric motor, then grew and churned through the water as first one, then hundreds of people rushed toward us.

She looked into my eyes, bowed her head and fell to her knees, the water lapping her chin. She clutched her son to her face. I reached out and placed my hand on her head.

Within moments, we were joined by the onlookers. Hands appeared from everywhere, reaching to me, touching me, pushing and pulling at the same time. I tried to step away but there was no escape. Faces and hands surrounded me.

I turned to retreat but lost my balance on the muddy bottom and slipped beneath the surface. I opened my eyes to hundreds of loving faces, distorted by the refraction of the lake. The bitter, cold water soaked through my clothing and poured into my mouth. I tried to find the bottom and push away, but the hands still reached to touch me and inadvertently held me beneath the surface. The more I struggled to reach the surface the more they held me down.

"Stop! I thought, "You don't understand! You're killing me, Stop!" I hadn't caught breath when I went under. Though I tried to keep from gasping, to hold on a few moments more and gain a foothold, I could wait no longer. My lungs demanded air and my body responded. I sucked lake water. The pain was excruciating. I tried to scream but only a rush of spent bubbles came forth and filtered through hundreds of fingers. I watched them rise to the surface and disappear.

***

I bolted upright in bed, cold and damp as if I had been in the lake and I gasped air like the boy in my dream. I grappled for the light switch on the small lamp and glanced toward the wind up clock next to the bed to see the time. Hopefully I hadn't wakened anyone. It wasn't quite five AM. I was exhausted but knew there'd be no further chance for sleep. My breath slowly quieted and I listened for the sounds of my neighbors. Apparently, I hadn't screamed this time, or they'd just grown used to my outbursts.

Two nights before, I woke from a nightmare around 3:00 A.M. As I tried to make sense of the surroundings I was shaken by pounding on the door. I'd forgotten where I was and when I tried to reach the doorway, tripped over a table and fell. The pounding increased until it shook the entire cabin. Someone demanded I unbolt the lock. I crawled across the floor, reached up and undid the latch to a rifle pointing in. I thought they'd finally come to kill me, however, it turned out to be a hunter, there for my rescue.

This time, I waited for a sound. When I heard none, I pulled the covers back and swung my feet from the bed. The floor was ice. My ankles began to ache even through the wool socks I'd slept in. The room was bitterly cold. Frost patterns reflected lamp light from the inside of the window. I dragged Levis and a sweatshirt from beneath the covers and put them on over my long johns, grabbed my coat from the top of the bed, added it to the layers and zipped it up. Finally, I wrapped myself in the old blanket I'd slept under.

I slid across the floor of the small room to the stove and lit all four burners for heat then placed my boots in the oven and turned it on low. I moved to the window and prayed for a hint of daylight to shake the lingering dream. Instead, a newspaper on the table caught my attention in the dim light. It drew me back to the nightmare as I looked at the half page photo of twisted, charred metal and smoking trees. I closed my eyes but the photo burned through and the lead-in snapped my memory back three days.

The Messiah is dead!

Jeremy Clay, believed by millions to be the Messiah returned, perished yesterday in a fiery crash. The helicopter that carried him plummeted into a hillside in a remote mountainous area in the Oregon Cascades. A local news helicopter witnessed the horrifying event in which Clay and his companions all died. Authorities are attempting to sift through the charred wreckage to recover any remains.

Spasms knocked me into a chair and I read the article again, the hundredth time in two days. The news helicopter came upon mine moments before the crash. They filmed the event for the world to see. Hours later, rescue workers reached the sight, but the remains were too charred to identify. The whole world watched as we all perished in a spectacular inferno.

I shut my eyes to squeeze the scene from my thoughts but it only intensified. Kathryn was dead, burned in the wreckage with the others. A tear padded against the newspaper and became part of the story. I wiped my face on the blanket.

The walls of the cabin seemed too close and I needed to escape before they suffocated me. After hiding here in near solitude for three days, I had to go outside or risk going insane. I pulled on my warmed boots, dropped the blanket to the floor, raised my coat collar and walked out the door. It was actually warmer outside than in the cabin. I made my way along the gravel drive that bordered several ancient, one room log buildings.

The 'resort' was isolated deep within the Cascade Mountains, hidden in the trees on the shore of a huge lake.

"God's Country", the guy had said. "It's kinda' hard to find. It gets busy in the summer, but this time a year, it's almost empty. Betty's got a little store there too. She stays year round."

It was what I had hoped for; a place to disappear, to sit back and consider what to do next. I needed a refuge where I could mourn Kathryn.

Indeed, it's been all that.

I stepped through the chilled darkness toward the lake. Pre-dawn fog made the entire forest nearly invisible. Although I couldn't see the lake, I could hear ripples wash the shore as I stumbled along the beach to the boat dock.

I made my way across the slick boards. The old structure heaved and sagged as I slid thirty feet on rotting planks toward the outer end, leaving the shore and lapping waves behind. With every vapored breath, the fog intensified. I couldn't believe how much the cold permeated from the dampness. Even in Michigan I'd never felt this chilled. Just months before, I didn't even know where Oregon was. Six months and as many lifetimes ago I lived with Ellen in Ann Arbor.

ONE

I opened the back door like a thief, not quite ready to face Ellen. I hesitated, took a deep breath and slipped inside. Jimmy Fallon joked from the television.

"Dammit", she was still awake. Inside the kitchen, I gently pulled the door behind me and closed my eyes as it shut with the harsh snap of the latch.

The sound stung my ears and I cringed. I'd hoped to steal into the bedroom and avoid confrontation. When there was no response, I began to walk quietly down the hall. Half way, I realized the absurdity and stopped, "For Christ's sake, what the hell is this?" I thought, "It's my damned house!" I threw my arms up, took a breath, turned and stomped to the living room to face her, angry that I'd acted like a guilty child.

Ellen sat curled in the corner of the couch, feet beneath her, hands in her lap. After four years I still lost breath when I looked at her. Her dark hair outlined and enhanced her beauty. It cascaded down past her shoulders and drew my gaze to the white, silk gown. She was small and firm and her hair parted gently around her breasts, almost as though she had arranged it that way.

She ignored me when I entered and continued to focus on the television. I stood in silence a moment, then walked to the couch and sat at the opposite end. I knew the peace couldn't last as I leaned forward to remove my shoes.

"It's a bit late, isn't it?" She snapped at last. I looked toward her and was captured by angry sparks emanating from her dark eyes. At that instant the TV audience broke into a loud extended laugh. I couldn't help but join them, shook my head and smirked.

"I told you to come. Donna asked where you were."

Ellen leaned toward me and spoke through clenched teeth. "I don't give a good God damn about Donna. Besides, she left at ten o'clock and it's after one now. You could have at least called to let me know you were going out." She fell back onto the couch and glared toward the TV.

She was strikingly beautiful when she got angry and lately, she was constantly gorgeous. I released a deep sigh. I simply wanted to retreat to bed but I knew I had to indulge her and deal with the pain tonight so the sore wouldn't grow and fester. It was late so I decided to attempt to reason with her.

"I told you Richard and I were going to stop for a drink. It was your choice to stay here. If you're bored it's your fault, I asked you to go."

I waited for a reply and realized my teeth had started to ache. My jaws were clenched and I'd stopped breathing. I opened my mouth and took a breath.

She continued to ignore me so I stood to leave.

"You never said you were going to a bar. If you did, I would have gone with you. At the very least, I wouldn't have been here alone in front of this damn TV all night, waiting."

I fell back to the couch. The gauntlet had been dropped.

She got louder, "The last thing I wanted to do was to sit there with Donna and her brats and drink airport beer. I can think of a hell of a lot better ways to spend my time. And waiting here for you isn't one of them."

Her anger grew and I looked away. My foot tapped rapidly on the carpet. I took another breath and attempted, in vain, to calm the situation, "Richard and I didn't go to a bar. We stopped at Alfie's, had a couple lousy drinks while we talked business, that's all. It would have been nice if you'd been there to say goodbye to Donna after all she's done for you. I thought you considered her a friend."

She stood and disappeared into the kitchen. I heard the refrigerator open, wine trickle into a glass and the door slam shut. She returned to the couch, curled back into her spot, took a sip then placed the glass on the window sill behind her.

Without warning she spun toward me and leaned forward on one hand. "Bullshit!" She shouted.

I jolted against the arm of the couch. She was furious but with the hint of a smile in her eyes as she raved.

"Where did you really go? Business hell! Richard hasn't got a damn thing to do with your business and I'm sure he couldn't give a rat's ass about bushes… Not your kind anyway."

She gasped and continued, "So Donna's out of town, I'm here alone so you two go out to get a little?" She leaned toward me now with both fists planted on the couch. Her eyes glared and I could sense her excitement. The air between us was alive.

"Find a little strange stuff tonight?" She harped.

It was her favorite game. I'd never cheated and she knew it. She accused me several times over the years. It was though she constantly wanted me to. I became fed up and decided to play her game. "That's it, Richard was lifting someone's skirt before Donna got through security and I slammed the woman with the wand while she frisked the passengers. Then we took the entire team to a sleazy little motel for a two hour pre-Easter gang bang. But hey, I'm home now."

Her voice screeched like a falcon as she attacked, "You son of a bitch! You really did screw someone tonight, didn't you? Tell me the truth!"

She bolted upright and held her hands as though they were prepared to strangle me. I couldn't believe she was serious. The entire scene became ludicrous and rapidly approached meltdown.

As she moved closer I grabbed her wrists. "Ellen," I shouted at her, "I'm really not in the mood for this shit. If I truly wanted to screw someone else, you sure as hell wouldn't be here."

I paused, looked deep into her eyes and spoke with quiet tenacity, "We live together. I made a commitment to you, for whatever it's worth. Despite what you may or may not think, I honor it." I paused "Sometimes I truly wonder why, but I honor it,"

Her anger faded and she sat back, ever so slightly. I realized that we'd played this game far too often and I was exhausted. I just wanted to escape and get some sleep. She looked confused as I pushed her arms away and stood to go.

She glanced toward the kitchen for a moment and then back to me. "What do you mean, 'for what it's worth'?" She jumped up and blocked my departure. "What the hell are you saying?"

"Ellen, it's late. Drop it. I have to get up early in the morning. I don't have the energy to play your damn games tonight. If you really want to do this, we can start over when I get home from work tomorrow and fight all evening. Right now, I'm going to bed."

I turned away from her and walked to the hallway. As I passed the television, I switched it off. The silence was intense; the only sound in the house was Ellen's angry breath. I escaped into the darkness and fell on the bed. The satin comforter felt cool and soft but the silence was obscured by the rasp of my pulse pounding in my temples. It sounded like fingernails scratching the pillow. I wondered if I would find sleep tonight.

Fallon's voice suddenly ripped the darkness open and I saw flashes of light as though I'd been struck by a shovel. When I realized it was the TV, I jumped from the bed and stormed into the living room. Ellen sat on the couch nestled in her corner. She glared at me, daring me to do something. The duplex rattled from the volume.

I went to the wall and pulled the plug. "What the hell is wrong with you? We have neighbors!"

"Fuck the neighbors and fuck you! I don't have to get up tomorrow. And if I don't sleep, nobody sleeps!"

I turned back toward the hallway, her screams followed me to the bedroom, "I'm going to Detroit in the morning. I need some time with Granny Frasier. You can sit on your ass and wait for me for a while. I'll go out and talk 'business'. I can talk 'business' all week long if I want to."

As I stepped into the bedroom I heard her move toward the TV. "Keep it down or I'll cut the damn plug off!"

Moments later muted laughter assailed the quiet as I pulled my sweater off in the darkness. I envisioned Ellen sucking the life from her Grandmother, the very woman who'd taken her in when she was thirteen and pregnant. Ellen claimed she'd been raped by her uncle although he swore he didn't do it. Evelyn Frasier found help for her and to this day Ellen denies anything ever happened. I stared out the window into the darkened yard as loneliness poured in to fill the room. It felt as though I was drowning and I fought for breath. I pulled my t-shirt up but it clung to the clammy sweat on my back. It finally came loose, I shivered and tossed it toward the closet. As I lowered my Levis, Ellen shouted again, "Jeremy! Come quick!"

"I'm sleeping!" I yelled and sat on the bed. I just couldn't start it all again.

"No, seriously, come here. Something's happening!" The flames were out of her voice and she sounded sincere. I took a breath, pulled my pants back up and reluctantly returned to the living room.

"Look", I started, "I'm done talking about this…"

"No, you look! Something happened again. They just interrupted everything on every station." Ellen stood facing the television.

The President's press secretary approached the podium and seemed extremely disconcerted. The announcer whispered an introduction and the secretary began to speak. I moved to the couch, picked up the remote and turned up the volume as she snatched it back.

"…to address the unconfirmed reports released earlier this evening. We have indeed, moved to higher alert status as a safety measure but our intelligence forces have found no present danger. We do, however, suggest all Americans remain vigilant and report any questionable activities. We've found no indication of threats to this country. Reports released by the media earlier tonight have not been corroborated. Your government will continue to evaluate the situation..."

The screen went dark. Ellen had turned it off. "Just more bullshit. I thought it might be something good."

"What do you mean 'good'? If it's such bullshit, why would they interrupt programing this late at night? What the hell are they talking about?" I stepped to the TV and pushed the button back on. Ellen immediately switched it off with the remote again and the light went dark.

"What's the matter Jeremy, afraid the terrorists are out there? After what you did, they just might be!" She laughed, turned her head and looked at me from the side with false threat in her eyes. "Donna's in Florida by now so if there weren't any plane crashes you don't have to worry. I certainly won't let the bad guys get you. You're mine tonight, all mine!" She laughed, started down the hall and stopped again. "I think I'm ready for bed now. If the world's about to end you'd better get busy. This might be your last chance."

She swayed down the hall, finger in the air, beckoning me to follow. I watched the white satin caress her hips as she moved. She stopped in the shadows at the bedroom door and ran her hand over her hip, shook her hair, then disappeared into the darkness.

I became enraged. I wanted to curse her and leave, walk out the door and never return. At the same time I wanted her to ravage me, burn off this anger and release the tension she hammered into me day after day. My body screamed for her and although I tried to fight it, I followed toward the few fragments of joy buried within all the shards of pain. I hated her and I needed her. She knew how to play me and I constantly fell into her trap. I punched my fist into my thigh but the need wouldn't subside.

TWO

Ellen was asleep when I left for work the following morning and gone when I returned that afternoon. I took a beer from the refrigerator, opened it, tossed the cap on the counter and slammed the bottle on the table. I sat and rested my head on my hands as bubbles rose over the bottle neck then slowly subsided. There'd been a chill in the air all day and cold beer wasn't as inviting as I'd hoped.

I leaned back, pulled the front chair legs off the floor and studied a crack in the ceiling then stretched and twisted my neck in an attempt to relax from the day's work and tension of night before.

News had been constant about threats of another attack. Some in Washington were adamant that investigations provided no justification for concern. Arguments and assertions continued throughout the day while the government sparred with the media and each claimed the other was irresponsible.

Despite the possibility of doom, my outlook improved when Ellen wasn't home to bury me under the weight of her rage. A sense of lightness flowed through me as I savored the silence.

When a car approached from the east and slowed, I grabbed my beer and pulled a large swallow, but the car continued on. The beer went down cold and bitter and I was reminded how much I dreaded her return.

My stomach tightened as another car came and went. The anticipation proved worse than coming home to her. When a third car got my attention, I reached for my phone and dialed Richard's number. It rang once... twice... a third time when he answered.

"Richard, I was hoping you were there! Hey, seems Ellen's on one of her quests again. She left me here alone. How'd you like to find someplace that cooks?"

"By 'cooks', do you mean fun or food? If you're thinking of dinner, I'm in. I just got home and this place feels like a cave. There's no mess, no noise! I can't stand it; I need to get out of here."

"I was hoping for some food. I've got Ellen, I can't have fun. Let's get serious! Maybe Chinese, Mexican? Hell, I'd even go for Greek?"

"It all sounds good. So...where *is* the light of your life?"

I ran my tongue across the front of my teeth as I thought of where she might actually be, "She said she was going to see her

Grandmother in Detroit" I swallowed loudly and bit my lower lip, "She'll be gone all week."

Richard took a breath before he spoke, "Should I ask how she got there?" He sighed, "I know we've been through this before pal, but you really shouldn't have to..."

"I know, Richard, I know. I kick myself all the time. Let's not even go there. She's an ass but she does have a few good points." I hesitated, "Actually, very few, but we have history and she needs someone stable. She doesn't know it but she really needs me."

An uncomfortable moment of silence passed before he continued and when he spoke his voice seemed far away, "Funny, I was looking forward to some time to myself. You know, I haven't been alone since before the kids. Nearly six years. God it's been a while."

He continued, "All day long I thought about what I'd do tonight, with my 'freedom'. Then I actually stayed at work an extra hour. All I could think of was last night, alone. I'm lost without them. I seriously need to get out of here. I sure wasn't looking forward cooking."

"Don't worry about it, Richard, it'll be better in a day or two, and when they get back, you'll be begging for a little personal space again."

I chuckled, "In the meantime, let's stop your loneliness and celebrate mine. I'll pick you up in about fifteen minutes. Figure out what you want, I'm starving. See you in a few."

I returned home at 10:00 P.M. to no one. Unlike Richard, I was relieved when my house was empty.

I undressed, climbed into bed and pulled both pillows together. I could smell Ellen on one and despite everything, it somehow soothed me. I drifted into sleep wondering whose bed *she'd* be sharing tonight.

THREE
KATHRYN

She stubbed her cigarette in the street, walked over and stepped into the revolving door. She was prepared for the confrontation but not looking forward to it. Yes, the boss was pissed off again, but he was always pissed off. He saw things exclusively his way, only understood what his pin prick mind could ascertain and that was usually fucked up and backwards. The Board had apparently been drugged the day they moved him up. He'd been a shit reporter, constantly stretching facts and sensationalizing events. His stories bordered on tabloid, but he'd somehow been promoted, most likely since he had a Bachelor's degree... in physical education, no less. He had certainly moved beyond his abilities because although he was a lousy reporter, he was a far worse editor. She imagined he felt fortunate to be in a position where could lord over the adults who disliked him, sure he'd grown up as the butt of every high school joke with no recourse other than to grin and bear it.

She nodded and flashed her I.D. at the guard in the lobby. He looked up from his desk and waved her in. As she walked by, she could feel his eyes crawl all over her. A gawker whose gaze could nearly sear a hole through a dress, he was as vacuous as the boss.

Others commented that he had "a thing" for her. As a man, he was questionable, as a guard he was worse, he didn't notice she'd flashed a driver's license rather than her ID, and even held it backwards.

The elevator opened, she entered and pushed number 17. She knew Doug wouldn't give her any credit, no one could please him. He had his idea of how things should be and no one, absolutely no one could measure up. He gave his opinion and always let the reporters explain their point and though he shook his head in agreement, he never heard a word they said. He was far too engrossed in whatever revelation he could impart next.

Kathryn knew she been delegated to his 'B' list and no matter what she did, could never move up to his "team of players". She cringed at that thought. The only alternative was to go over his head and file a complaint but she figured he must have connections to stay in place as long as he had with his failing record. He was apparently an 'excuse' man with all fingers pointing toward his staff. Fighting him at this point could lead to corporate suicide. She decided to listen to his drivel and wait for the proper time.

He would eventually be identified as the problem and the shithead would be discovered. Someone above was bound to realize his lack of worth and that he was a major reason the magazine was stagnant. She only hoped the day would come that they fired his ass before the magazine fell to far. Everyone's life would be better if he weren't there.

In the restroom she checked to confirm nothing was out of place, nothing personal he might focus on. She hoped to discuss his issues, his inane requisites, to focus on performance, not appearance. He often became totally absorbed with insignificant details; a twisted collar, a skewed clump of hair and would make that his target. He was so fucking anal.

In the mirror, she smoothed her hair and checked her makeup. Prior to leaving she viewed a full reflection and was satisfied there was nothing that might distract him from her work.

When she entered his office, he stood, greeted her and waved her to a chair to sit. But then he sat on the corner of his desk and towered above her.

Her smile was cold and almost angry as she looked up and did her utmost to refrain from telling him to "go fuck himself".

"Kathryn, welcome back. I appreciate your taking valuable time to come up and see me." He leaned forward and she worried he might fall from the desk and land in her lap.

"I was hoping that we could celebrate your return, in fact, I planned to take you to lunch, however, we still seem to have the same problems we discussed last time. I briefly scanned your work and even though I thought we had an understanding, you gave me more monkey shit, nothing but palpable monkey shit."

Kathryn forced a civil smile. She wanted to slap him off the desk but knew he took pleasure invoking reporter's anger and refused to amuse him.

"The research is solid, the writing is strong but I see nothing but information. And you know I want more. I want the monkey's claws. I want something that's going to dig into a reader's skull and force him to read to the end. I want him dying to read it over again, to obsess on it, to have nightmares, damn it! When people read this magazine I want them to worry about tomorrow. You need to add a frigging hook. People can get the facts anywhere. We want more! For God's sake we *need* more. We're a dying breed here. We need to shock the monkey till he screams."

He smiled, "And I know you can do it. You won two Gossamer awards your first year out. You either had natural talent or they taught you how to use all those hooks at that God Journal. I believe in you. I'm sure you know how to push the reader's buttons and scare the hell out of them. Instill some fear, that's all I'm looking for."

"Listen Doug," she stopped to breathe and took a cigarette from her purse. "I won those awards for writing, not for 'lunatic baiting'. If you recall, I also won awards at Ford, Hillman and Stanley well after I left, as you call it, the "God Journal". And all for the same work I'm giving you! After all, isn't that why I was hired here in the first place? Have you ever gotten complaints from above?" She started to light up.

"What the hell do you think you're doing? You know you can't smoke in here."

She studied him with contempt, "Open the window, that's what you do when I'm not here." He glared at her. She took the cigarette from her mouth and put it away.

"Kay," he continued, "I know how good you can be. You have great possibility, that's why I'm trying to work with you. No, no complaints...not yet! Frankly, it doesn't matter if the Board likes your work or not, I decide what our readers get, and you work for me. You'll write what I want, when I want it and the way I expect to see it, is that clear?"

She was quiet for a moment. Thoughts raced with responses that would shave the fat from his bones. She could have him bawling uncontrollably in the corner in fewer than three minutes, flat, ego gone and totally destroyed. Instead she replied in an investigative tone, "So you're asking me to 'create' news? Fantasize stories based in fact? Is that what you're saying?"

"Kathryn, Kathryn, Kathryn," he became even more condescending, "Don't even suggest those things. I know you understand. I'm talking artistic license here. I want facts, but you need to be a bit more creative with them. For God's sake, no one wants Sergeant Friday anymore, 'just the facts, ma'am'." He smiled, "remember him?"

"You want to be a bastion of truth, I applaud you. For God's sake I encourage you, but try to add a little Steven King to the mix. I'm not suggesting fiction, we're a damned news magazine after all, were in the business of facts. All I'm saying is spice the shit up a bit! Try to sell the God damned story. We're here to stay alive and make money, for Christ's sake."

"OK Doug, your point is that you want me to add a touch of horror to my work. Just how far do you want me to go? To what degree do you want the readers splattered with blood?"

He beamed at her apparent acceptance, "That's what I'm talking about, lay it on. Let yourself go. If it grabs me, it grabs our readers. If I think you've gone too far I'll let you know. We're trying to take 'market' here. If Fox can persuade the nation that Geraldo is a war correspondent, I know I can make you into a "color" reporter."

She lowered her head and looked up at him with a gentle smirk, her rage invisible. She glanced over at the desk beside where he sat, took a quiet breath, gathered her will and spoke softly, "If you truly want sensationalism, I'll give it to you."

"That's the spirit! That's what I want to hear. Just let your artful side take control. I bet you'll like what you find... and believe me, it'll improve the team's attitude. Remember what they say, 'happy boss means happy employees!' "

"Doug, I'd like to add one condition, a request, if you will. I'd like to receive some more significant assignments. Give me something with substance, something relevant. Allow me something with importance and I promise you'll get your monkeys. You'll have monkeys clawing their way out your ass."

He continued to smile but his eyes gathered into a tight squint. He glared at her as she politely waited for his reply.

**

A short while later, she sat across a table from Tom at Vincent's Lounge nearing the bottom of her third glass of wine. "I swear, if he could have read my mind he would have choked to death on the spot." She tapped an unlit smoke end to end on the table. "They would have found me dancing on his desk."

Tom was distant, he seemed indifferent, "I just don't understand why you let him bother you so much. You fought like hell to get this spot. Screw Doug! Write his way and keep your career. If you appease him, maybe he'll offer you something respectable instead of the crap he sends you on. He might even let you cover things here in the City. We'd have more time together."

"Tommy, what the hell are you saying? I write news not soap operas! I still have *some* integrity, for God's sake. Do you think I should throw it away for that jackass?"

"I'm just saying you're capable of doing what needs to be done. Satisfy this cretin, make him happy and in time, it will work out." He raised a finger above his shoulder for the waiter, "You're a writer, that's the key. What difference does it make what you write? None of it matters if he fires you? Give him his trash and continue your career."

The waiter arrived and Tom pointed indifferently at his empty Martini glass and tapped it as he continued, "If you're that dissatisfied, put feelers out. Find something better. I'm sure other publications would love to give you a break, but in the meantime...write and be happy!"

"'love to give me a break'? You think I need a break? Listen Tom, I've worked my ass off to get where I am. I've earned it! I developed a style that's won awards and that asshole wants me to compromise more than ten years of integrity."

The waiter watched as she continuously tapped an unlit cigarette on the table then asked if she was ready for another glass of wine.

"No thank you", she smiled and nodded to him before she continued, "I'll lose any chance of growth if I produce the shit he's demanding. There are fewer than six publications at this level and they're all in association. If I compromise here, nothing I've ever done will mean anything. I'll be finished."

She tipped her glass and drained it. "The only publications that would even talk to me are the trash rags. And you find that acceptable? You of all people!"

"Kathryn, he's not asking you to write about space ships or Bigfoot." he smiled dourly, "We both know you're not Edward R. Morrow. Frankly, I see Doug's point here, magazines are fading and the old crap just doesn't sell today. The public wants flash, something to draw them away from their computers. The old school is passing away and it wouldn't hurt to give in a little. I'm sure he knows what he's saying. Do you truly believe he would risk the magazine and his own position?

He finished his Martini, turned his back to see the waiter and spoke as he waved his glass toward the bar, "I personally think you're making too much of this. So the guy's an asshole, he might just know more than you're willing to give him credit for. Besides, if the result allows us more time together, what's the problem? I'd suggest you give it strong consideration before you react." He finally caught the bartender's eye and waved his empty glass again. When he turned back the table was empty but for a crushed cigarette in an empty wine glass.

***

She reached for her pack and realized her jacket was still draped over the chair but didn't bother to look back. She stepped to the curb and hailed a cab. She decided to leave it and Tom.

FOUR

The following Sunday I woke around nine, uncommonly late for me. The back yard was alive with birds, their songs carried by the daylight through the window. I lay back and closed my eyes. Remnants of a dream lingered and I tried to recapture it. It was intense and important. There was something about an intelligent, determined woman. I'd known joy and warmth and true love. I tried fiercely to retrieve it, comprehend the essence, but the entire episode seemed to evaporate in the sunshine. As hard as I grasped to hold on, the feeling followed the night into yesterday and was gone. I got up, pulled on some sweats and left the dream to fade beneath the sheets.

In the kitchen I emptied old coffee grounds into a sour smelling trash can beneath the sink, parted the curtains and opened the window. A breeze filled the room with the scent of spring. I heated the small burner on the stove and filled a pot with water for tea.

I unlocked the back door and pulled it open then barely pushed the screen. It swung wide and slammed the wall with a crash. Birds flitted into the trees and hid among the leaf buds. As I retrieved the morning paper, sunlight filtered through branches. I retreated and left the door open to welcome May in.

I floated two teabags in a mug of hot water and sat at the table to read the news. Headlines still repeated the possibility of a terrorist threat. Debate had been hot the previous week with the media demanding the government act while the President denied any concern and encouraged everyone to go out and shop. Several news stations, apparently trying to enhance May ratings, claimed we were doomed while others sided with the President, offering that he'd exhibit more concern if a threat actually existed. Homeland Security kept a surprisingly low profile and fed the press nothing, leaving them to their own imaginations.

The previous evening Richard said, "It was a huge mistake. Someone overreacted and now they're paying for it." He smiled, "Do you think Washington would purposely set the country on edge and then give us nothing?"

He continued, "If they suggested New York was about to be hit again they'd have to deal with nine million people trying to escape Manhattan at the same time."

I scalded my fingers as I pulled the teabags from the mug and squeezed the remaining water from them. I drew a sip of strong tea that went down hot and burned my throat.

As I blew into the cup to cool it, a pickup came down the road and stopped in front of the duplex. Through the window, I saw Ellen step from the passenger door and present an exaggerated, vengeful smile toward the house.

All my joy vaporized and left a thorny pressure in my neck as though a ninety pound vulture had dug its claws into my shoulders. My back began to throb and each breath seemed to weigh me down further. The spring morning became thick and heavy and the peace I'd felt dried up and withered inside me. She went to the other side of the truck, said something to the driver then leaned into the window. I turned back to the table and glared at the newspaper but try as I may, I couldn't make sense of the words.

The engine revved and tires burned as the truck roared away. When the annoying noise faded into the distance, it was replaced by a far more irritating sound of footsteps on the driveway.

She pulled the screen door open and it slammed against the outer wall as she entered. I continued to stare at the paper. She stopped in front of me and stood in silence. The door slammed shut with the sound of a shotgun.

"Miss me?" she taunted and stepped closer. I looked up without comment. She held her overnight bag in both hands and gently swung it back and forth in front of her hips.

She greeted me with an even more caustic look, "Granny says 'Hi'." Her smile pointed at my throat with revenge glistening on its blade. She was primed for a fight, looked as though she already smelled blood and craved more.

I glanced back toward the paper, "Didn't know your grandmother drove a truck."

She let go a razor chuckle, "She was upset that I came alone but I told her all was fine. I just needed to get away from you for a while. I can't understand why the old girl worries about *you* so much. She knows how much you piss me off."

She leaned close and whispered, "She thinks it's wrong when I stay out all night, but I told her you're O.K. with it and you do the same thing?" She snorted.

When I didn't respond, she started toward the hallway, but stopped for more. "I'm going to take a nap, haven't had much sleep this week." She paused, anticipating anger, but instead I quietly stared at the paper while she continued to wait.

When I finally did look up I realized I'd been bludgeoned by her so often my fury had just rolled over and died. It became a vapor somewhere deep within and drifted away on my breath. I studied her for any indication of what could possibly have kept us together all these years and realized whatever had existed was now gone. I searched her face to find something; anything; the love, beauty, the desire I'd seen in her just the other evening.

She looked like an empty canvas, blank and without detail. I saw nothing but an ugly, pathetic stranger. She seemed to realize a difference in our dynamic. Her acrid smile dissolved and there was question in her eyes. We shared the silence a few moments longer when I saw the slightest hint of fear touch her. She stepped back with an awkward motion and slightly moved her lips but said nothing.

Within moments she quickly jumped back into her typical arrogance where anger and hostility defeated any doubt. She shook her hair, offered a defiant scowl and appeared ready for the games to begin again as she firmed her back, raised her shoulders and waited for me to respond.

I was blank and felt nothing but wonder. I tried. I just looked at her, searched for something intriguing, anything, but there was nothing left. Nothing at all. I shook my head in disgust, returned to the paper and this time, began to read.

She waited again and when I still didn't react, turned and stomped toward the bedroom, shouting as she went, "Wake me up around one!" The door slammed behind her.

I got up, walked to the sink and gazed out the window. The bright spring morning was now dull and sallow. I knew in my heart that this could go no further, she'd have to leave. I felt immersed in profound emptiness. Though I was finally able to breathe again, everything I knew was about to change. My life had been dragged to a frightening depth. I stared blankly through the window, hoping for the next step, the next moment. I was at the very bottom and wondered if I would rise up.

***

A phone rang somewhere in the distance, soft at first, but it crept into my consciousness and grew louder and more defined with each pulse. It was on the table behind me and on the fourth ring I grabbed it. At the same time, Ellen threw open the bedroom door and shouted, "Answer the damn thing already."

I ignored her. It was Richard, at least it sounded somewhat like him. The voice was weak and fractured, entirely wrong. He spoke softly, in clipped sentences without meaning.

Ellen continued to yell from the hallway. Though I couldn't understand her words either, I shouted back, "Would you shut up?"

I realized he might think I was talking to him so I pleaded, "Not you Richard, I'm here...what's wrong?"

"Fuck you!" Ellen screamed. She slammed the door and continued in a muffled screech.

I returned focus to Richard. He'd just continued talking in a voice low and raspy, shrouded in black, "...dead, Jeremy. I think they're all dead. It's all over the news. I think they're dead..." He began to sob. It grew into a deep choking sound, as though someone were crushing his throat. I shouted into the phone, "RICHARD! RICHARD, are you there?" I still heard the choking but it was more distant. "Richard, if you can hear me, I'll be right there. Hang on, I'm on my way."

I turned it off and dropped the phone on the floor where it bounced noisily. I didn't stop to pick it up but ran to the bedroom to get my keys. When I opened the door Ellen was in bed and rose on one elbow. "Don't you ever talk to me like that. I'll say whatever the hell I want, this is my house too."

I ignored her, grabbed the keys and rushed out. "Where do you think you're going?" she demanded. I scooped up my phone as I reached the back door and heard her shout, "Don't you dare walk out that door!"

The screen door slammed open against the bricks as I rushed through. Before it banged closed again I faintly heard her voice following, "You damned well better talk to me you son of a bitch."

I jumped in my car and started it. As I threw it into reverse, Ellen reached the door.

She wore only panties and bra but she was covered in rage. She screamed something at me as I gunned the car out of the driveway into the street. I stopped just long enough to slam the transmission into drive and look back toward the house. Ellen came after me, shouting something.

She shook both fists in a surreal, animated gesture that would have been hilarious at any other time. She neared the car and reached for the door handle as I slammed the peddle to the floor. I last saw her in the rearview mirror, nearly naked in the street, flipping both fingers at me as I drove off.

FIVE

I raced through the streets of Ann Arbor. News of the destruction of a coastal town in Florida coursed from the radio. A small nuclear device had been detonated from the top of a 23 story building and had obliterated a square mile of Cape Sardis. Initial reports said that everyone in a three mile diameter had died. The headquarters of Martin Spencer, a defense contractor and a leader in drone technology, was the apparent target.

The entire area had become radioactive. No one was allowed near the city. The President, who had just assured the nation another terrorist attack was completely unfounded, was able to respond instantly and attempted to declare national Marshal Law. He immediately closed air space across the country, dispatched Navy and Coast Guard ships along the Florida coast and had military forces ready and in place to isolate all highways leading into the state. Underneath reports of the destruction, questions were rising about how a massive military presence was available and in position if there had been no advance warning.

Cape Sardis! During the years I'd known Richard, I'd come to hear quite a bit about the city. Both he and Donna grew up there and met through their fathers who had worked together for more than 20 years. Several other family members were employed at Martin Spencer as well. They loved the sun and the sand. No one could understand why Richard wanted to move to Michigan when most people followed the opposite path.

I'd met their parents one year when they all visited Michigan for a white Christmas. Of course it didn't snow that year, but they were wonderful people who accepted me as family. We still exchange Christmas cards.

"My God," I thought, "What'll Richard do next Christmas?"

A horn brought my attention back to Ann Arbor and I swerved to miss a car I'd just cut off at an intersection. In the rear view mirror I saw the Buick slide sideways to a stop. The light I'd just run was bright red.

I stepped on the gas and continued toward Richard's house. Several people at a bus stop were huddled together, all fixated on their phones and notebooks. They stood motionless, like a group of cardboard cut-outs.

A police car passed in the opposite direction, lights flashing. I thought about the Buick and wondered if everyone had indeed been O.K. but still didn't slow down. I realized I should have called 911 before I'd left; help might have gotten there quicker.

I sped up and fishtailed around the corner at Edwards Street, tires squealing. The car slid but I keep it on the road the final block and a half to Richard's brick two story. There, I braked and lurched toward the drive, bounced over the curb and stopped on the lawn just short of the porch. I pushed the car door open, jumped out and ran up the steps.

His front door was locked so I pounded with my fist, shouted and waited a moment. I realized my car was still running on the lawn and glanced to see the driver's door hanging open. I turned back and pounded the door again. There was still no response so I slammed my fists even harder. With no sound inside, I backed to the edge of the porch and rushed forward with my entire body, striking the wood with all of my weight. The catch shattered and the door crashed open.

In the living room I stopped, unable to move further.

Before me was Richard, wrapped in a robe, unshaven, rocking back and forth. He knelt on the hardwood floor, haloed in the light from the television. The TV was on but no sound came from the speakers. News people spat out silence, as though their voices had been dislodged. They were like fish in the bottom of a boat, gasping for answers.

The house phone laid sideways, a dead soldier, beside him. It was silent, lifeless, beyond messages demanding he hang up, past pleading screeches signaling circuit extinction. The only sound came from deep within Richard, a constant escaping breath, shaken lose from his soul. He didn't even respond when I burst in. I don't believe he knew I was there. I felt as though I'd entered a nightmare. I wanted to turn and leave, even return to Ellen. At least she was a known misery.

The entire scene was far worse than I had imagined but I had to be here, needed to be here to help somehow, to fix things. I tried to go to him but my legs were like rubber.

I spoke softly, "Richard?" He didn't seem to hear me. I spoke louder, "Richard!" Still, there was no response other than his gentle rocking back and forth.

I was finally able to force myself closer, placed my hand on his shoulder and spoke again, "Richard, its Jeremy."

At my touch, he stopped bobbing and slowly turned. As he looked up, my heart seized and my breath failed. Hollow, lifeless eyes gazed blindly through me, beyond me, toward the ceiling. His demons clawed their way up my spine and punctured my heart. I shuddered uncontrollably. Before me knelt a man without a soul, an animate body with no life spark.

Acid churned from my stomach and I swallowed back sour

bubbles. The room became fuzzy and ill-defined as I stared at him. I grew unsteady and collapsed by his side. The impact of my knees cracking on the floor jarred back a hint of clarity.

I threw my arms around my friend and we supported one another. Each bracing the other from the fall.

SIX
Kathryn

"Kay," He grunted into the phone, "I sent you to Florida for a specific story. You might not see the merit, but it's what I want and what this magazine needs."

She shot back, "Doug, what the hell? Can't you understand? I'm right here, 60 miles away. This is the biggest story since the towers and you want me to cover some damn love triangle?"

"Kay," he spoke as if to a child, "You haven't earned those rights yet. I have Martin on his way from Virginia as we speak. And we have three local contractors already on site. You need to stay focused on this NASCAR issue. I've got space reserved for it."

NASCAR hell. Two drivers shot by one of their wives while they were porking each other? What kind of shit is that?"

"Kay, it's what people want to read. It's shocking, it's curious, it's appealing. You promised you could get colorful. So go for it, get colorful. If you'll get off your horse and do what I tell you, then we might look at more significant assignments. Right now I need you to bring me something with teeth. NASCAR is huge and this *story* is huge, Kay…"

"Don't call me Kay you fat ass bastard,"

The sound of a helicopter chopping the air made her statement break up.

"What was that, Kay? I didn't quite catch that last thing."

"Kiss my ass, Doug. I quit."

She threw her phone in the front seat of the car, lit another cigarette and started to get in when she realized it was a military unit landing on the emergency pad at the top of the hospital. It was greeted by a rush of medical personnel so she stepped back to the parking lot, dropped her smoke and ran toward the building.

SEVEN

A semi passed on the right and drenched the car with filthy water. The windshield wipers smeared mud and made the road nearly invisible.

"Damn it!" I sprayed the window again and tried to see ahead. My right turn signal flashed incessantly.

Each time I tried to move from the center, another truck cut me off and drenched the car with more mud. Everyone who approached from the rear cut past me on the right and prevented my lane change.

I shouted, "You son of a bitch!" as it happened the tenth time.

Richard remained silent the entire drive from Ann Arbor. Though my nerves were frayed and raw, I couldn't begin to imagine how he felt. I'd been raving most of the trip while he just stared into his lap. He'd been in survival mode since the attack.

I finally stepped on the gas and forced my way in front of an Escalade when it tried to cut me off. The driver laid on his horn and jerked back to the fast lane. He flipped me off as he went by, followed by several more cars within inches of one another. They were close enough to be attached. It amazed me that these people survived this madness every day. With a commute like this there is no wonder Detroit drivers are all pissed.

I despised this insanity and got involved in it as seldom as possible but Richard and I were to attend a memorial service for local families of people killed in Cape Sardis. It was a national day of mourning and there were more than a hundred thirty people expected from our state alone.

I'd spent the past few days taking care of Richard. He refused to see anyone or leave the house. We were inundated with constant attempts by news people to invade his space. I agreed to run interference and keep the media at bay. I offered a simple 'No Comment' over and over, but finally had to go as far as to threaten some insistent journalists with a bat when they wouldn't quit.

Word of the memorial services was released and I insisted Richard attend. At two AM I moved my car to an adjoining street. At six, we snuck out the back, over the fence through a neighbor's yard and escaped in silence.

Windshield wipers sang a monotonous dirge on top of the stillness in the car. I'd turned off the radio because every station blathered about the inevitable retaliation. They almost universally called for a nuclear war. My car was equipped with a dead, antique cassette player so silence was our only other option. I'd hoped the trip would cause Richard to finally open up and say something. Despite the weather and the traffic, he still wouldn't respond. I thought maybe, if I could make him angry, he would, at least, feel something.

"I can't believe Singleton said this was "God's punishment". He's the definition of a terrorist, trying to devastate everyone. He's basically saying, if you don't agree with him, you don't deserve to live. He might not have killed anyone but he sure incites people to do it for him. I think that son of a bitch should be hanged for treason."

I waited for a reaction but Richard didn't even blink, just stared toward his lap. I exited the freeway, headed north and reconciled myself to silence for the remainder of the trip.

We approached Bloomfield Hills some twenty minutes later and I pushed the car through a yellow light. I was becoming more and more stressed and I just wanted this journey to end.

The bad weather and the horrendous traffic intensified my anxiety and Richard, who'd always been animated and vocal, made the situation all the more surreal.

I turned left at the urging of a miserable voice from my phone. It had been a long morning. Finally, a sign announced the chapel ahead and I felt a huge sigh escape. "Your Destination is ahead on the left." The voice announced so I signaled and entered a turn lane.

As I waited for the green arrow, I realized Richard was considerably different from who he'd been a week before. He'd had a future then. I asked, "Are you going to be alright?"

He turned toward me and I shuddered at the void in his eyes as he whispered the first word since leaving home, "Sure" he simply stated then slowly returned his gaze to his lap.

The light changed. I pulled into the long drive leading to the chapel and for some reason, began to tremble.

The tranquility of the setting drew me in and calmed me slightly. The road ambled through acres of gardens, bordered by huge oak trees. It was a classical, timeless design, a landscape masterpiece. We passed fountains and statuary as we approached a huge stone building. Serenity warmed my chill and the tremors began to subside.

I'd always dreamed of creating something this passionate, this beautiful. Something more than a lawn for an apartment complex or business park. We entered the parking area and proceeded to the far end. Although we were early, a crowd was already waiting.

I looked at Richard who still sat in silence. He didn't seem to notice we'd stopped.

As I pulled into a space, the crowd rushed toward the car. They all had TV cameras and microphones. We were instantly surrounded by talking heads with a barrage of muted questions. We were assailed before we exited the car.

I pushed my door open and several bodies flowed back. As I stepped into the swarm, I was surrounded by voices, stinging me from all sides. I made my way to the front of the car and attempted to reach Richard's door. The crowd had mobbed too close and he was unable to get out. In unison they all focused their attention on me. Microphones appeared from all angles and a din of voices surrounded me, each trying to overpower the other. I couldn't reach his door handle and Richard sat in silence, trapped in the passenger seat.

"Stop!" I shouted toward the mob, but their mouths continued to drone unintelligible questions. I moved away from the car and some followed. Others stayed on guard in case Richard should exit.

In the distance uniform bodies rushed toward us. I raised my arms as though I was drowning, reaching for a life ring and cold sweat dripped down my sides. My confusion turned to anger. I grabbed one person by the collar and demanded, "Enough! What the hell is wrong with you people? Get away from me!"

Four escorts from the chapel pressed through the sea of reporters and formed a wall between us. Two others cleared the car so Richard could exit. We were united again and what seemed the leader of our cavalry shouted toward the crowd. I heard "civility and private property" behind me as the contingency led us toward the chapel.

As we climbed the steps, without warning, Richard stopped and turned to the reporters. I tried to continue to safety but he clutched my arm and held me there. He glanced sideways at me and imperceptibly nodded his head. I saw the first sign of life in him since the disaster. He held up a hand and spoke quietly. Some still shouted questions but they too finally fell quiet so they might hear.

"My name is Richard Sandberg. S-A-N-D-B-E-R-G. Easter Sunday, I lost my wife Donna, my two children, Tyler and Heather, my Father, Mother, my Mother's sister, my wife's parents, her Sister and Brother in law and their three children. Anything beyond that information is personal and your questions are an affront to decency. Please let us mourn our families today. This is our time. Allow us some semblance of dignity."

He turned and proceeded toward the church. The din began to rise once more when a single voice cut through. "Mr. Sandberg?" Richard continued walking, the guards and I followed close behind. "Mr. Sandberg, are you related to Maggie Donavan?"

Richard froze in mid step. His eyes opened wide and he spun toward the voice, mouth open, unable to speak. He looked at the woman in silence.

"Were you aware that Maggie Donavan is still alive?"

EIGHT

Three hours later, after the service concluded, we escaped the media circus and followed the reporter through several side streets and highways across to Woodward Avenue and a private room at the Kingswood Inn.

We parked, hidden out back in the employee lot and entered through a rear door. Kathryn Lawson offered to buy lunch and update Richard about the status of his aunt for the price of a "brief and painless" interview. She had done her homework and already had the room reserved with the intention of securing a meeting.

I quietly watched as they spoke, a miniature tape recorder centered between them on the table. I was a bit anxious about her intentions.

Richard leaned forward, transfixed on information about Maggie. A faint semblance of hope touched his expression the first time since the disaster.

Kathryn explained "I was in Orlando doing another piece when the bomb went off. They'd found Maggie a couple miles from the blast area, alone, wandering aimlessly. She was in severe shock, apparently, they dragged her into a military helicopter and airlifted her to South Seminole since Elgin was filled with Air

Force and corporate people, anyone significant to Martin Spencer who might have been nearby.

"Your aunt had burns on her hands and face. She was barely able to breath from all of the dust in her lungs and she'd been severely irradiated. They say she'll recover from the burns but I'm afraid they've done everything they can as far as radiation poisoning. Richard, I'm very sorry to tell you, she doesn't have much time."

Kathryn reached down, pulled a cigarette from her purse and began to tap it on the table.

He looked at her and his breath stopped a moment. "Where is she?"

"As I said, I was about to do another interview at the hospital when the attack took place. I decided to follow the event."

She hesitated, a faint smile appeared in her eyes and she looked to the celling as she remembered.

"I was about to leave, but by the time I got off the phone with my editor a military helicopter landed on the roof. I had one foot in the car when an emergency team surrounded the helo. I went back to gather information and made my way nearly to the landing pad just as they wheeled her in. Everything was crazy and everyone was distracted, so I flashed my creds and followed along. They had no idea if I was supposed to be there or not. Your aunt was conscious. I was able to talk with her while they took her to emergency. I offered help as they rolled her through the door. Of course, they wouldn't let me follow and made me wait outside."

She reached for his hand, "I waited. I waited five hours until they stabilized her. I got to know the desk nurse quite well and when they took her to a room, she told me where. I attempted to see her again but the doctor refused to let me in. That's when I started to raise hell in the hallway. Your aunt apparently heard. She was scared to death. She remembered me and told them I was her daughter."

She smiled softly, "They didn't have any idea what the hell was going on. There was no direction. The chopper left a single, low rank Airman to monitor the situation without instructions. He was glued to the desk phone trying to find someone who could give his some sort of instruction."

"By then, almost everyone in the hospital was exhausted since no one had reported for shift change and several others had slipped out to be with their families. The place was nearly empty and the remaining staff was running around trying to take care of the patients. It was crazy so they agreed to let me in to see her.

She looked Richard in the eyes, "Maggie was terrified, she had no idea what had happened. No one told her anything. She'd been grabbed by the military dragged into a helicopter and dropped at the hospital without so much as an explanation. She thought it was the end of the world. The Bible. When I told her about the bomb, she wouldn't believe me. I think she would rather it had been some religious ending instead of an attack by human monsters.

She was devastated and talked nonsense for a while so I held her hand until she calmed a bit and finally gained some composure. We started discussing her family in Cape Sardis. That's when she mentioned there were people visiting from Michigan."

Richard became visibly shaken so she stopped to allow him to contain himself.

He nodded and she went on, "She said she'd had dinner with your wife and kids the night before. She wants you to know your entire family bragged about you."

She took another moment, swallowed, then continued, "It was about that time the guard came back. He exploded and started screaming for the desk nurse. When she came in he told her to get me out of there because if they knew I was talking to his prisoner, they'd bust his ass and throw him in the brig. He was in her face and he said, in no uncertain terms, he'd be sure she got fucked too."

She tapped her cigarette harder until the tip split and tobacco began falling out, "When he called your aunt a prisoner I knew I had to do something."

She looked at the unlit cigarette and put it in her pocket, "The desk nurse told him to get the hell out of her patient's room. She said, 'You can't threaten me in my hospital', slapped him hard and ran out. He went after her.

"I didn't even have to think, I got your aunt up and we found our way through the service doors and out to my car. She hid in the back seat and I got the hell out of there. We passed an Air Force security van just up the highway."

She continued, "All I can say is that she's safe and doing the best that can be expected."

Richard sat back, "Prisoner? How the hell could they call her a prisoner?"

"I'm so sorry to do this to you here...now." She reached over and took him by the shoulders, "I tried to talk to you in Ann Arbor but every time I called, some crazy man refused to give you the phone, and when I finally flew here he met me at the door with a baseball bat."

My face began to burn and Richard almost smiled. She sat back and let him go.

"So, how much time does she have?"

He put his hands back on the table and looked down.

"Six months at the outside. She can still function but the doctor I'm working with said she'll experience more pain every day and it won't be long before she's bed ridden. She wants to see you again."

His eyes widened as she continued, "We can make that happen but it won't be easy. If you'll promise exclusive rights to your story, we'll blow this thing apart. The more we find out, the more she wants the world to know what the bastards did to your family. We think we can put a face on this and allow people to see how horrible it all is, how it actually affects everyone."

She took a deep breath, "This fight about marshal law and who's actually in charge is to our benefit, the chaos in Washington is our best friend."

Kathryn wouldn't offer details but seemed confident she could unite Richard and Maggi. "I've got some high level government supporters who've offered to help. Politics being what it is, there are those who want to get whatever ammunition they can to further their agenda."

I grew more anxious and uncomfortable by the moment. It felt good that Richard might see his aunt, but the talk of prison and government infighting was well beyond my comfort. I wanted to rescue him and take him away from this crazy person. On the other hand, it seemed almost reasonable to get up and leave him there with Kathryn, walk away and try to regain some sense of normalcy.

***

With an agreement forged, Richard and I returned to Ann Arbor to await Kathryn's directions. Rain had stopped and we now traveled post-lunch, pre-rush. Richard's demeanor had improved slightly and although he was still quiet, at least he occasionally acknowledged my comments and even cursed a driver with Ohio plates when a car cut in front of us across three lanes to an exit.

We spoke little as one city faded into the next. Signs for Ann Arbor finally appeared and we both became despondent as we left the freeway at Main. We drove in silence, turned onto Richard's street and approached his house.

I pulled into the drive without conscious attention, stopped the engine and felt in my coat pocket for the business card Kathryn had given me. I pulled it out and looked for hope as I removed the key.

Richard said, "What the hell?" I looked to see him gape out the windshield, wide eyed and astonished. I followed his gaze to the front lawn. I was stunned. I opened the door and stepped from the car. There in front of me, strewn across the lawn, the sidewalk and the porch, was everything I owned.

A tangled mess of clothing was mixed with my electric razor, duffel, landscape tools, a bag of fertilizer, CDs and more.

The rain had turned everything into a mass of soggy garbage. I stood frozen, unable to believe what was before me.

I barely heard the passenger door slam as moist footsteps approached. A hand clasped my shoulder and I realized Richard was at my side.

"Son of a bitch!" were the only words I could muster.

"What do you think?" Richard said with a chuckle in his voice, "She trying to tell you something?" He began to laugh.

I was enraged! Now, everything I owned lay in ruin. After all I'd done for him, he somehow found humor in my loss. I gradually turned to see this mad man laughing at my distress. My expression must have bordered on absurdity because the moment I faced him his laughter grew so intense he nearly stopped breathing and had to lean on me to keep from falling.

The neighbor next door stepped onto his porch and watched stoically for a moment, wiping his hands on a dish towel. Richard saw him and choked for air. I held his arm to keep him up and shook my head as he delighted in my pain. He convulsed with laughter and I realized I was beginning to smile as well.

He took several deep breaths, pointed toward his mailbox and squeaked, "What the hell is that?" then collapsed to his knees, nearly hysterical as I dropped his arm. I wouldn't hold him any longer. I coughed, lost my breath and burst into a donkey bray that wrenched my throat.

I stumbled through the soggy mess, slid on a sport coat and nearly fell backwards. At the mailbox I pulled out a wad of papers, all envelopes addressed to me.

I shouted, "They're bills!" and dropped several on the porch as I bent to catch my breath.

"She seemed really angry." The neighbor called.

Richard fell, face first into the wet grass, choking with laughter. Bubbles popped from his nose in the lawn. My eyes watered and I tossed the rest of the envelopes in the air. They fluttered down to the garbage covering the yard. I staggered down the steps and sat beside my friend and roared helplessly until my every muscle ached in agony. It had been far too long since we'd hurt with joy.

NINE

The following day airwaves were filled with breaking news that a rebel organization known as the Islamic Militia of Pakistan was tentatively identified as the architects of the attack on Cape Sardis.

In the previous year and a half, the excessively militant arm of al-Qaeda, in an attempt to unite several tribal areas from adjoining countries, had wreaked havoc and mass murder against those who opposed them. Nations around the globe called for an end to their vicious bloodshed but when each affected country was attacked and attempted to respond, the militants simply escaped across a border. Although the locals were relentlessly threatened, each nation refused military incursion by their neighbors, claiming attacks on their soil would be considered an act of war. That effectively gave the IMP political asylum within the lands they were devastating. The militants consisted of only 700 soldiers but they were somehow equipped with the latest technology and weapons, and were said to be highly funded. No country in the region had the capability to stop them.

After thousands were murdered and the stability of the area

was undermined, the U S House of Representatives demanded America step up. President Conrad conceded and authorized drone strikes against the group as they took refuge in Pakistan.

In response, the Pakistani government filed grievances with the United Nations Security Council, stating the attacks threatened the sovereignty of their country and were illegal. Though condemned by the Council, President Conrad intensified strikes when the affected nations refused to work together and end the terror.

The UN filed formal objections but when Cape Sardis was attacked, they became suddenly silent. Tensions flared around the world as nations, shocked at the extent of the brutality, feared total nuclear war.

The Security Council immediately called for restraint and filed a resolution pleading with the United States and Pakistan to allow time for them to interpret the intelligence and develop accords for a united front before any acts of retaliation.

The world waited.

TEN
Kathryn

"Dammit Kathryn, I'm getting killed here. What in God's name have you done? Friggen FBI agents are camped in the file room. They're investigating us for Christ's sake."

"Doug, do they know I don't work for you? Did you tell them I quit because of your obnoxious fat ass?"

There was silence for a moment. Doug continued in a muted tone, "I've left message after message for you. You need to return my calls."

"Doug, what in God's name would make you think I'd want to talk to you? I only answered this time to tell you to leave me alone. Get it through your thick head, I've quit. I don't work for you anymore. Face it and quit bothering me. I'd appreciate if you'd just go away. I'm on to bigger and better now and I don't intend give you any of it."

He continued, "Kathryn, I know you were thinking of leaving but hear me out, please."

She sat in silence a moment as he continued, "I talked to the board. They want you to stay," he hesitated, "so do I. Besides, they said that since we didn't have a formal, signed resignation, you're still ours."

She exploded, "Like hell! If the board thinks they own me or any of my work they'll have to fight me in court. I've already quit, damn it!"

He sounded as if he were about to blubber, "Kathryn. It's not just you. They called me on the carpet. I admit it, I screwed up. You were right there and I should have worked with you but I sent someone else in. I need you to understand, if you refuse to cooperate, I could lose *my* job. They're serious here."

He continued, "I had no idea you had something big. They actually called me incompetent for dropping the story. They just want to know what it is you've done. You've apparently scratched some raw nerves with the military and now the entire board is being investigated. Homeland Security is in our house for Christ's sake. They want to know everything about you, where you are and who you've been talking to. You did something that made them very angry and they want payback. I promise, the board will protect you but you've got to agree to resurface."

"Are you serious? Do you even hear what you're saying? You son of a bitch, you refused to piss on me and now that I'm driving the rats from the cellar, you ask me to come back?

He suddenly shouted, "I'm not asking you, dammit, I'm telling you. Don't even imagine this is a request. It's a God damned legal order. Do you understand?"

"Too late, Doug, I've invested a shitload in this situation and if you think I'm going to come back there and give it to you, you're delusional. This is my future and seriously, you can wipe your ass with that tabloid from Hell. I'll never come back."

There was another silence. She could sense his grinding jaws and narrowing eyes. He wasn't used to being defied by one of his minions.

He finally let go, rage grating in his voice, "You listen to me. I have a contract with your signature on it. It says I own you and everything you do while you're with this magazine. You *may* have mentioned you quit and maybe you didn't. It's your word against mine and trust me, mine holds a shit load more weight than yours. Until I receive proper notice, written notice, formally signed and notarized, you still work for me and this corporation. I want what you have and I want it now, understand?"

She laughed, "Don't bullshit me. You've made it perfectly clear over and over again that these jobs are 'at will'. You've threatened to fire us at any time for no reason. 'At Will!' That, my dear Dougy, goes both ways. You owned my work until the moment I quit. Tell your board of directors that you fucked up, fat ass. You're the one that cost them this. I wouldn't share it with you for all the money in the world."

She chuckled, "And while we're at it, since I'm sure they're listening, Hey, FBI or Homeland, whoever is monitoring this, Doug is responsible for whatever comes out. I won't give anything to him but when the shit hits the fan, I'll point all ten fingers and all ten toes in his direction. Might as well take him away right now, before the coward makes a run for it"

His voice softened, "'Kathryn, come on, I know we've had differences, but it hasn't all been bad. I need your help here. All I know is that everyone suddenly wants to kick *my* ass. I'm getting heat from the big guy. Not the managing editor, not the board, but Murdock himself. He and the President are blood brothers. Something huge is going on here and we're not supposed to look. If I don't get a handle on this I'll be a pariah. I'll be castigated for everything I've ever done since puberty. If they fire me I'll have no recourse. There's no place I can go. I'm not the one demanding this. Please, I need your help."

"You know Doug, I could almost feel sorry for you, but I don't. They just want what I have to censor it. Tough shit fat man, ain't going to happen. Tell them if they try to fuck with me I'll hold nothing back. I have some devastating information and I have options and there are a lot of people out there behind me, big players."

She knew she had the upper hand. There was no more than a personality piece but they didn't know that. She'd saved a 'prisoner', an innocent witness to nothing. The government wanted Maggie, wanted her bad without knowing why. There was definitely something amiss, they seemed to be running scared.

Doug took a breath and continued, "You don't understand, they've got me and my family over the blades. I'm sure you won't be surprised to know that I've had a few, somewhat seedy instances in my past. People I thought I had in my pocket have come back to bite me. This is dangerous business. I'm asking, no, I'm begging. Please help, if not for me, for the sake of my wife and kids."

He sounded like a beaten man but after all his bragging, harassment and threats she just couldn't feel remorse.

He softened more after his confession, "So, can I tell them you'll come in? Do this for me and you can name your future. I swear we'll cover all your expenses to date and I'll give you whatever you want, nothing but the cream of the stories."

Kathryn sat at a table in an outdoor café as she spoke to him on a prepaid phone. She lit a cigarette, inhaled deeply and sat in silence as wisps of smoke disappeared on the breeze. When she took another drag she noticed a waitress approaching who looked upset. She dropped the butt on the sidewalk and crushed it, placed a five dollar bill on the table and left.

ELEVEN

The real estate broker placed the coffeepot back in its stand and passed me a ceramic cup. I nodded graciously and took it but it was extremely hot so I quickly placed it on a magazine.

"Are you sure I can't get you some?" He smiled at Richard who shook his head and waved the man away as he looked over the papers piled in front of him.

The man turned to his office window and raised the blinds. "Days like this, I just have to let the sunshine in." He returned to the table, eased his weight into the chair and smiled toward me. Sunlight brightened the room and highlighted the gray in his hair. He dressed well, though not wealthy.

He appeared to have been in the business for quite some time. His office was worn but comfortable. Awards and posters adorned the walls and photos decorated his desk. He had a sense of achievement over the sale of Richard's house.

I tried to calculate the commission in my head when he spoke again, "We were darn fortunate with this one. The market's been flat since The Cape. Everyone seems to want stay put for a while. The Bentons were getting pretty desperate before you put your house up. They've been living in an extended stay hotel since he transferred here. They were feeling the pinch." He smiled, "You must be thrilled to close this quick?"

He waited for Richard's response and when none came he blinked several times and smiled toward me again. Richard picked up an ink pen, signed a page and shifted it from the pile in front of him to another on his right. He began to read the next document.

We'd been in the office for nearly an hour and my comfort level was beginning to disappear. The man was obviously thrilled about the sale, however, he was not aware of Richard's motives.

He started in about the bombing of the Cape and talked of a nuclear response. "That damn Evans is siding with the United Nations and wants us to hold back. Hold back hell, I hope we nuke the entire Middle East. We should just get rid of those bastards once and for all."

Richard didn't look up. I just wanted to change the subject but yawned deeply, thanked him again for the coffee and took a quick gulp.

Hot liquid scorched my mouth and I nearly spit it back. Instead, I swallowed and it burned all the way down. I clamped my eyes shut and cursed under my breath. When I looked up the agent watched me with one raised eyebrow. Although he said nothing, it seemed he wanted this to end as much as I did.

***

I emptied the cup for the second time, leaned against the window sill and watched cars drive by. Richard signed the final document and handed the entire stack to the man.

"I just want you to know how happy the Bentons are with this. I assure you they'll take very good care of your home." He reached his hand to Richard and they shook, then moved to me with his hand still in the air and pumped my arm.

He continued, "If you're ever in the market for another house, just give me a holler. I'll find you a place that's just right and make the process as pleasant as possible. Remember, I'm full service here."

I offered a polite smile and nodded, he glanced at the cup in my hand. I handed it to him and he placed it in the sink on the wet bar.

***

Richard planned to meet Kathryn in Virginia. Florida turned

out to be an impossibility. Apparently, when the Air Force lost charge of Maggie, it was believed she may have escaped with unknown, restricted information and so was currently considered a fugitive. The government had determined Kathryn's identity but with multiple investigations encompassing the IMP and their possible connections, she and Maggie were considered a minor threat, albeit an unknown matter of possible national interest.

Kathryn's current plan was to move Maggie to Virginia to a secure location between the Sunshine State and Washington DC, away from the clusters of military and Homeland Security in both locations. Kathryn assured Richard she would have them together soon. It was difficult to imagine she could coordinate it at all with the entire country on alert but she felt the massive confusion to be a benefit.

***

Papers were all signed and we were about to leave when it hit me, I'd soon have nowhere to live. Moving back to my place wasn't even a consideration since Ellen had apparently squatted there with someone else.

"Excuse me," I said. The agent changed focus and was

instantly animated, ready for another opportunity. "Actually, I could use a place to rent. Do you have rentals?"

"Hmmmmm." He looked at the ceiling as though he might find an answer written there. "I really don't," he said, "But…There's a lady who works in the office with a place about to come open next month. I think it's in Chelsea. I could talk to her for ya', get some details. If it interests you, I could probably work out a good deal."

We shook hands, exchanged information, then Richard and I left the office. June was just arriving. I stopped in the parking lot to catch a breath. "How ya' doing?" I asked. Richard had become gaunt and pale over the past weeks as his plans to go to Florida decayed. He didn't sleep and often woke me as he paced his house. The only food he managed was what I put together and basically forced on him.

He shrugged and proceeded to the car. The move would either create a new beginning or leave him alone and on his own. I tried to get him to wait for word from Kathryn to be sure things would work out, but he refused. He needed to leave behind reminders of what had been and as much as I hated the thought of losing his friendship, I couldn't help but feel he'd be better off somewhere else.

As I pulled the door open and slid into the passenger seat, I tongued strings of blanched skin that hung from the roof of my mouth. Although the coffee had been hot, it was lousy, hardly worth the aggravation. My entire mouth was scorched so I was grateful for the lack of discussion as we returned to Richard's, or what had been Richard's house.

We drove along in silence through the old neighborhoods of Ann Arbor, passed the houses, lawns and gardens where Richard and I became friends. They no longer seemed welcome or comfortable.

Across the country, millions of people hid behind walls of wood and brick and prayed there houses might be an island of safety in this sea of fear.

I glanced at him as he drove along familiar streets. He was a different man now, quiet and removed. He existed somewhere deep within, only faintly aware of anything that surrounded him.

He'd gotten rid of everything but a few clothes and his car. We entered the driveway next to a huge red and blue sign that screamed "SOLD" in large white letters. When the engine stopped, neither of us moved, we sat without a word.

"You know?" He said at last, "We'd had a lot of plans for this place. It was our dream home. Now it's my nightmare."

TWELVE

I shook the underwear from my left foot, stepped into the tub and slid the shower curtain closed. Water poured from the tap as I lifted the faucet, and when the temperature rose, I made adjustments until it flowed soothingly hot.

I pulled the knob on the spout to redirect and listened as the moisture surged through the pipes. I closed my eyes as it began to shower down from above.

The warm spray surrounded me as I tipped my face down and drew a deep breath of steamed air into my lungs to wash away the dust. Dirt, sweat and tension flowed down the drain.

I squeezed shampoo into my hands and returned bottle to the shelf but it lurched and fell. As I grabbed for it, I missed and caught air while it dropped to the tub below. Plastic clanked on enamel as it bounced and I tried to recover it but slipped and fell against the wall. When I grabbed at the faucet as I fell it inadvertently slammed shut and water stopped flowing. I slid beneath the spout in an awkward, uncomfortable position and lay there listening to hollow gurgling in the pipes.

There was no blood and nothing broken so I started to get up when my hand, still slick with shampoo, slid across the enamel and this time I banged my head hard on the tub rim. Sparks filled my eyes and my ears began to ring. I lay back to regain equilibrium. The tub was cold against my skin and all I could imagine was being in a sitcom with a live audience watching, pointing and applauding my finesse.

I crawled to a sitting position and pulled the faucet open to rinse my hands. After a moment, when nothing came from the spout, I cursed my clumsiness. I'd apparently broken the damn pipes!

I began to rise when a faint sound, like steam bubbling through mud, came from somewhere deep within the wall. It grew louder so I slid back to avoid being scalded but no water came.

As I watched, gas spurts burst from the spout and splattered some sort of rusty looking spittle with each pop. It smelled as though it came from the cesspool. I slid back further and tried to get out of the tub, gagging from the stench. With a sudden loud gush, thick, red-brown ooze erupted. I stood up but as I tried to exit, I slid in the mess and this time I fell through the curtain, toward the toilet.

***

I opened my eyes and realized I was on the bathroom floor. Stabbing pain throbbed incessantly in my head. The cool tile felt good against the headache and I would have stayed there but I was cold and naked and the smell from the pipes made it difficult to breath. I pulled myself up and looked at the tub. The bottom was filled with thick red sludge that reeked of a rotting corpse. I nearly gagged and began to heave. I had to get away since I was about to vomit. I grabbed the vanity and realized my hand was still coated with shampoo, although it was now thick and nearly dry. It made me wonder how long I'd been unconscious. I toweled my hands, pulled on my pants and a T-shirt from the floor. As I opened the door, hinges grated and old wood scrapped against wood. It sounded like a casket from a horror movie. It seemed to open harder than normal and I was struck by the sense that something other than the headache was extremely wrong. I stepped into an odd warmth in the hallway and gasped for air.

The smells of spring had somehow become fall. All was desperately awry. Chills climbed my back and I stopped a moment to gather my senses.

I pressed my hands on my temples to try to end the throbbing but it didn't help, so I limped toward the living room where I was assaulted by another rush of nausea. I stopped to balance against the wall and squeezed my eyes tight but the pounding wouldn't subside. After a moment, panic began to grow and I had to continue. Everything was hazy so tried to rub dust from my eyes but it didn't help. As I passed the bedroom, a breeze fluttered the curtains and at the end of the hall it struck me that something was desperately wrong. I strained to understand what it was when I realized the windows were all open and I hadn't left them that way.

I stopped again to listen and wondered if someone had broken in while I was unconscious. There was no other rational explanation. Someone might still be in the house. The floor squeaked as I stepped forward. My breath seized and I fell back to listen for a response, a movement, breathing, anything. There was only silence underlined by rustling curtains. I leaned forward and peeked around the corner.

The living room was empty but the TV and stereo were still in place. My fear didn't diminish, something was still frightfully wrong. I just couldn't comprehend what it was. I finally gained the courage to move forward, slowly, prepared for a fight. As I looked around, I realized the haze wasn't from my eyes, the entire house was washed in an odd jaundiced light. Was it sunset? Had I been unconscious that long? I looked toward the front door and that window was open as well...No! It couldn't be. The glass in that door was fixed. It was somehow missing. Curtains flapped in an odd warm breeze. The entire floor was powdered with shards that sparkled in the yellow light.

I went in and fell back on the couch. My head pounded. I searched the room and I tried to understand what had happened but just couldn't focus or comprehend. My stomach churned. The smell from the tub hung faintly on my clothing and mixed with a sweet burnt odor. I began to cough and nearly vomited so I rushed to get outside. The stench of death filled my lungs and made me gag. I pulled the door and hit the screen on the run. My hand went through the mesh and I stumbled out, breaking the staves, leaped down the steps where I fell to my knees and heaved.

When it was over, I froze in terror at what looked to be the edge of eternity. The entire world was shrouded in a dense cloud of opaque, yellow dust. Sunlight barely filtered through and made the diseased air glow with a dingy pall. As I breathed the thick, burnt smog, my lungs filled with fine ash. I began to choke and pulled my T-shirt over my nose and mouth. I became lightheaded and had no idea what to do. I wandered toward the front gate and the street to escape. Everything was wrong. There were no cars, the road was deserted. My skull continued to pound with each step. I wiped my forehead and grit scratched my skin. I realized I was covered with yellow-gray ash.

When I reached the gate, the world seemed deserted. My headache, the smells and disorientation overwhelmed me again. I leaned over the fence and heaved until my stomach was empty. Weak and barely able to stand, I decided to call for help and find out if I truly saw this or if I'd scrambled my brain in the fall.

I turned back to the house and looked across the yard. Neither the trees nor the bushes had leaves. To the north, as far as I could see, everything was scorched. The front of my house was blistered and blackened. I could no longer move. I couldn't breathe. It felt as if I were about to die and I collapsed to the ground.

I jerked awake from the fall. It'd been another damn nightmare. Another specter from Hell. I turned on the light and sat up in bed shaking.

THIRTEEN

My phone battery was nearly dead, however, it lasted long enough for an irate customer to burn up the air while he chewed me out. I pulled up to the office park where I'd dedicated the past two weeks. The August heat was relentless and I hesitated to move from car's air conditioning into the misery. Parked at the curb, I finally stepped out onto new blacktop. There was no shade anywhere and the glare of sun caused the street to shimmer with waves of heat. My shoes sounded as though I'd stepped in gum as I walked over the fresh asphalt. Mosquitoes circled my head and one stung my neck. The dirt and sweat burned as I slapped at it. The swarm wasn't at all bothered as I attempted to swat them away; they just continued to buzz around me and attack.

I tripped over the curb and when I caught my balance, reached down and pulled the skeleton of a bush from the ground. It came up without resistance in a puff of dust. The sprinkler system apparently failed. Thousands of dollars of plants, trees and bushes had baked to death in a matter of days.

I threw the leafless hulk against the building's brick wall and the root ball exploded in the heat. A cloud of dirt seemed to hang forever in the still, hot air.

I kicked at a shrunken strip of brown sod, curled and lifeless on the ground. The three acres of lawn that I could see were a patchwork of death.

I went to the vacant building and sat on new, white concrete steps. It felt like the entrance to Hell as the sun beat down and the mosquitoes persisted in their torment. I was as ruined as the landscape.

My business was young and my reputation expanding. I was nearly ready to hire help. This contract would have given me the security I needed. It would have put me over the top. Now it appeared to be my demise.

Another mosquito stung my arm and as I swatted it another flew into my ear. Frustrated, I slapped at it hard. My ear rang through the pain. I smacked my arm again and looked down at two large splotches of blood, drawn out by the devils then crushed from their bodies. I stood up to get away from the incessant swarm and inspect the sprinkler control. When I rounded the back of the building I saw a twenty foot circle of green lawn and heard the sound of water dripping. As I approached the entrance to the utility room, I noticed where dirt was turned next to the building. There was a line cut through the dead turf extending back toward the road. It was extremely obvious because water had followed from the circle along its route. The gash was damp and muddy and there was green along its length surrounded by dead landscape. Someone had buried a wire to the building and cut my water line.

I was instantly enraged at what I found but relieved at the same time. On one hand, some asshole had cut the line and left my new landscape to die, on the other hand, they would pay for my losses.

I followed the cut to a utility pedestal at the edge of the sidewalk. For Christ's sake, they couldn't have hit the line and not noticed. From the cut, a stream puddled over the curb, down the gutter and into a road drain. I shook my head and wrote down the utility information.

My cell was as dead as the lawn by now so I returned to the car, found my charger and plugged in. I started the engine to make calls but before I turned off the radio, another special announcement began. I stiffened in the seat prepared for the worst.

> Reports are reaching us that joint forces from the three neighboring countries, plagued by the IMP took actions to seek out and destroy all members of the organization and associated followers of the group. The nations, Pakistan, Afghanistan and Iran

leveled a coordinated attack from all three countries and now claim they have eliminated any further threats.

Several leaders from the organization, including three members of the Saudi Royal Family who are believed to have funded the group, were taken into custody and publically beheaded. The executions were televised throughout the Middle East. The United States has just agreed to stand down and has removed all consideration of nuclear retaliation.

President Conrad and his father have been close friends with The Saudi Royal Family. Questions are emerging about his relationship with those who funded the bombing and if he dismissed any forewarning for that reason.

Senator Evans of Washington State has demanded an investigation concerning vastly contradictory messages from our intelligence organizations and the Executive Branch to determine if there was deliberate lack of action leading up to the Easter disaster.

He said, "If there is evidence that information was mishandled and the attack was allowed to happen through misconduct, we will take appropriate steps to be sure a situation like this can never happen again. We will investigate every possibility, up to and including the highest levels of our intelligence forces and the executive branch of our government."

He continued, "Disclosures have prompted an inquiry into possible links between funding of IMP by the Saudi Arabian Royal Family and their interests in Interglobal Aeronautics who have been in competition with Martin Spencer for US Government contracts."

My dead landscape seemed less of a disaster considering what might be going on at the top levels of our nation. Nuclear war had been diverted but it wasn't over yet. The investigations might yet, tear this country apart.

The news continued.

"In related breaking news, more than two hundred bodies were found this morning in Simmons, Texas where an alleged cult is reported to have committed mass suicide this past week. In a video left at the scene, the victims were seen dancing a 'dirge', crying and shouting for forgiveness.

"They denied suicide and claimed they were preparing to join the meek at the right hand of God. Apparently their actions were in response to several statements made by evangelist Reverend Singleton who made claim we are seeing the beginning of the prophecy from The Book of Revelations."

He was a lunatic but I wondered, if possibly, he might be right.

FOURTEEN

"They just had no idea." Richard repeated again. He grinned as we pushed through the mass of people at Dulles airport. I'd arrived that morning from Detroit. A surprise call from Richard came three days before to invite me to the "party".

Since parking at the airport was overwhelmed, Richard had taken the Metro to get as close as possible, then cabbed the remaining distance. We'd spent the remainder of the morning surrounded by exasperated crowds in constant flux as we waited for Maggie to arrive. I would finally meet the woman whose name had now gained national attention.

It was wonderful to see Richard again, now that he too had become famous. He'd grown his hair longer, had a slight beard and covered his face with large sunglasses so he wouldn't be recognized. In this crowd, I couldn't imagine anyone being identified. Kathryn's blog had gone viral making him and Maggie the spotlight for an entire movement. His image and an old photo of Maggie appeared everywhere. His comments were still reported as though he were somewhere in Michigan. Accompanying stories of their losses and finding one another had been picked up by every media outlet and they'd become central figures in the appeal to expose the facts behind "The Cape". He was driven by a new force and seemed alive again.

Some hoped to silence him so Kathryn forced him to give only phone interviews from an Ann Arbor cell number, in fear for his life. She produced and directed everything around Richard and Maggie's thoughts and statements.

As we weaved and dodged the throngs, Richard mentioned speculation the president might have had some collusion with the Saudis and Interglobal. It was difficult to believe he had failed to prevent the carnage but evidence was mounting.

"That jackass needs to be behind bars if even half of what they're suggesting is true," I said, "Even if he isn't responsible, if he didn't do anything to prevent the bombing he should spend the rest of his life in Gitmo, albeit a very short life."

Somewhere, from within the confusion, shouts arose. Noise flowed through the crowd like a wave. The entire throng began to roil as all movement stopped and people attempted to determine what was happening. A sudden, shrill scream brought silence and several people dropped to the floor while others tried in vain to escape in every direction, all blocking one another.

The shouting stopped as quickly as it started and the disorder gradually calmed. People stood from the floor, looked around in embarrassment and acted as though nothing had happened as the crowd continued to shuffle along. We looked at one another in disbelief. The entire country was still terrified and nothing seemed strange any more. We continued toward baggage claim to find Maggie. Her plane had arrived on time but the massive crowds had delayed us.

"Will you recognize her?" I asked Richard, "It's been a while and you said she doesn't look like those photos anymore?"

"She said she'd be the only bald woman on the plane." He smiled sadly.

We finally made our way to the carousel for the flight from Atlanta. Crowds were massed in the area.

"Damn it!" Richard searched faces and slapped the railing. "We'll never find her in this."

I glanced at the countless bodies surrounding us though I had never met the woman and had no idea who to look for.

Kathryn had taken Maggie to a doctor she knew in Jacksonville who tended her wounds until she could travel. They smuggled her into Georgia and put her on the flight from Atlanta under an assumed identity. It was all very covert. I was amazed they could secretly get her on an airline with all the tightened security, but apparently, Kathryn had developed incredible connections who intended to accomplish something huge.

Richard dialed the cell Maggie had been given but it rang without an answer. We certainly couldn't page her. We were bringing her in under the radar and the government was still interested in what she might know. Richard jumped on a bench to look through the confusion.

Through the hum of people a voice called out, "Over here." An arm waved above the mob.

"Richard," I shouted, "there." and pointed at the hand moving slowly toward us.

Within moments they embraced in tearful reunion.

She carried only a few personal items so we proceeded through an endless procession flowing to and from the parking lot.

I smiled at Maggie, "They're here for the rally. You did this. Both of you."

She looked around stoically, "I sincerely hope we can make a difference."

"All these people might well be on our side, but they're going to screw up our plans if they don't let us through." Richard took Maggie's bag and pushed his way to the shuttle. We passed the cab stands crowded with passengers waiting for nonexistent rides.

Some forty minutes later we were finally second in line at an auto rental window to pick up our 'preferred, no hassle' car.

The man in front of us was extremely sharp with the service agent. Apparently, there were no more cars available. He raised his voice and when that didn't produce results he began to curse at her. The clerk smiled a practiced, frozen smile and assured him that the supervisor would find some way to assist him.

She asked him to step aside to wait while her supervisor came to find a solution. He called her a "fucking, worthless bitch!" and stomped off.

The woman behind the window took a breath, raised her finger to suggest we wait, picked up her phone and whispered something extremely pointed into the receiver. A moment later her practiced smile returned and she addressed Richard with forced pleasantry, "Can I help you?"

We left the lot stuffed in a Kia Rio that fortunately, had just returned. We passed the angry man as he waited in line for a nonexistent cab.

That evening I watched Richard and Maggie across a candle lit table. Her appearance was somber. Only a small patch of hair remained at the base of her skull and her face and arms were covered with scabs that looked extremely painful. It was amazing she could function at all with what she must be enduring. Through all else, her eyes didn't seem to belong. They sparked life; fiery and overflowing with excitement.

Ironically, Richard was the opposite. As he talked about the coming rally, his eyes were milky and flat, almost as though he was the one preparing to die. "So, Kathryn has arranged for us to speak at the demonstration just prior to Senator Evans. Apparently he plans to release some critical evidence they've discovered in the investigation into the Saudis and Interglobal. He wants to release it to a worldwide audience.

They want you and me to affect the emotional side of the event and create deeper support for their information. They've acquired evidence on how the IMP got the bomb into the United States. The entire program is designed to continue developing the movement to end this madness and expose those who've been responsible for it."

He looked at her, "I'm so glad you're here. I'm so sorry…"

She allowed a painfully sad smile, "Do you mind if I talk about it?"

We each looked at one another in silence until Richard said, "Not at all."

Maggie told about being with Donna and their children at the 'big house' as they called it. The home had been in the family since the beginning of the 20th century.

She spoke about leaving dinner that evening. "We hugged and said our good evenings. I had to go home but I was going to return for the kids Easter egg hunt the next day. I was preparing for bed." Her memories seemed overwhelming.

Richard took her hand, "You don't have to."

"I need to," She said, "When I try to hold back, it devastates me. I'm afraid I'll lose control." Her eyes widened, "If you're OK?"

He nodded, she squeezed his hand and continued, "Richard, my place is…was in the country, north of the Cape. Everyone else, the entire family, was in the city."

"I was in the shower when it happened, apparently just far enough from the center. I think the bathroom tiles, the tub and water protected me. I hit my head when the explosion shook the house. It knocked me out. I don't know how long I laid there. When I came to, ash was everywhere. I ran outside but could hardly breathe. Everything was burned and dead. The air was yellow. I thought it was the end of the world and I was in Hell."

A butter knife rattled against my plate. I looked up to see everyone staring as I trembled uncontrollably.

FIFTEEN

The following evening, the sun set bloody red, creating an eerie, wounded landscape along the highway. I welcomed the darkness, took a turn at the wheel and drove Richard's car north with him and Maggie. Kathryn left separately early in the morning to mislead anyone who might follow her.

We had talked and prepared throughout the previous night and most of the morning. When we left Richard's apartment in Virginia that afternoon, I realized how tired I was and tried in vain to nap.

Now my turn to drive had come too soon. I spoke over my shoulder through a yawn, "Maggie, you should get some rest. It'll be a while before we get there and I'm sure there won't be another chance until this is over."

Her answer came unexpectedly sharp, "Don't worry about me! I'll get all the rest I need soon enough." I looked at her in the mirror, bit my lip and said no more.

Richard was silent, fidgety and angry. I was relieved he finally let me drive since traffic was extremely heavy as we closed on DC.

"Looks like the Mall's going to be packed. I guess everyone wants to beat the crowd." No one responded.

We continued in silence. Anticipation the night before mixed with lack of sleep had morphed into aggravation. Everything began to feel very wrong when several miles from the Capitol, traffic came to a complete halt.

"I don't believe it." Acid climbed in my throat as I inched forward and braked, forward and braked, again and again. No one said a word. I wanted to pull over and get out, but the shoulders of the highway were lined with cars that had already done that. They expected us this evening so we had no recourse but to continue since Richard and Maggie were the key surprise speakers. There was a huge chance that they would both be detained and questioned when they left the stage but Kathryn had assured them that it would all be caught on camera for the world to see. They were fugitives for no apparent reason, the world loved them and wouldn't let them be bothered for long.

Excitement had long since eroded and the monotony of the trip became surreal and hollow. Deep in my gut an incessant shudder kept telling me I shouldn't be here but I convinced myself it was just nerves, exhaustion and the Big Mac I'd had an hour before.

"Look out!" Richard threw his hands against the dash and I slammed the brakes as a car cut in front of us from the shoulder with inches to spare. We were hardly moving but Richard bounced forward and Maggie hit the back of his seat.

"Goddamn..." I turned to see if she was hurt and heard the dull thud of metal against metal somewhere in the distance behind us. "Are you alright?" My seat belt caught as I strained to see.

She slid back in the seat, holding her forehead, "I think...I'll put my belt on." She pulled the seat belt across her shoulder and it clicked loudly then sat back.

"Maggie?" Richard looked at her through the dim light. His eyes were wild, animal like. My heart pounded in my ears. I burped acid and swallowed it. I wanted to leave the car right here and walk home.

A horn honked and I looked to see three car lengths in front of me. Maggie spoke abruptly, "Everyone's in a hurry, just drive. I'm fine!"

Richard turned back and stared out the side window. I moved the car forward and filled the empty space.

The following fifty minutes inched us closer to the Capitol.

Lights flickered on the Mall, slowly growing larger as we

approached. They were the tip of a shining sword that split the blackness in two. It seemed like an eternity before the sword became the Washington Monument.

My feet ached and my head throbbed when we finally reached the point where I was to turn. Exhausted park officers directed traffic. The man we approached was rumpled and looked as if he had spent his life at this spot, waving a car from one direction, then another. Each driver stopped to ask questions. He shook his head, waved into the empty sky then pointed this way and that. I began to tap my fingers on the steering wheel.

I wanted to honk the horn or rev the engine to get his attention but realized it would probably just piss him off.

Our chance finally came nearly 10 minutes later. As I passed within two feet of the patrolman, he looked at me through the window. He must have been drained but he nodded pleasantly and smiled. The tension eased. "We're here," I said with a sigh. My passengers still said nothing.

Richard sat up as we passed hundreds of people on foot. In front of us, looming through the night, we were accosted by brake lights once more. I gritted my teeth and leaned out the side window to see what the delay might be. It was just the mass of people and cars moving toward the site.

We drove forward a few yards when we suddenly stopped again. "Damn, I'll be glad when this is over." Heartburn bubbled up even more. The irritation was becoming painful.

We inched along until we came upon a wall of teenagers stretched across the road. They laughed wildly and passed a bottle back and forth. The car in front of us followed them a few minutes, then finally pushed its way through. The group immediately closed the gap and blocked our way.

I tapped the horn two times quickly. They acted as though we weren't there. I moved closer, but they didn't budge.

Richard opened his window, thrust his head out and screamed "Get the hell out of the way you self-serving bastards! Move your asses or we'll run over them!"

I was shocked. I'd never heard him threaten anyone before. The teens acted as though they hadn't heard and continued in mass. Richard shifted his weight and thrust his foot to my side. He tried to stomp the gas pedal and scraped his shoe down the length of my shin.

"What the hell are you doing?" I shouted. At once I knew, the engine screamed and the car lurched forward. I threw both feet on the brake and pushed with all my strength. One boy dove for the shoulder without even a look. The others turned and scrambled out of the way. As we passed, a cigarette hit the windshield. Sparks splattered red like blood across the glass. The remaining ashes almost looked like a bullet hole. Richard muttered obscenities under his breath and glared straight ahead. Maggie never said a word.

He finally moved his foot back and I drove forward slowly.

SIXTEEN

We finally reached the parking area where a man with a flash wand and an orange vest waved us to his side.

"Sorry folks, but there's no more space here. You'll have to make your way to the exit over there." He pointed toward tail lights in the distance.

"But we're supposed to speak tomorrow. They told us there'd be space here tonight. This is Maggie Donavan." I waved my hand over my shoulder.

He shined his light in the window and leaned over it. He smiled and his face lit up in a soft orange glow. A moment later he backed out and searched the papers on his clipboard, "Donavan, Donavan...Here you are, Richard and Maggie." He looked back in, 'Sorry about that. There's just too many people here. You need to find Randall Thompson. He's in a trailer over behind the grandstand." He pointed toward several lights across a field.

"Just a second, I'll get someone to flag you." He pulled a radio from his belt and spoke to a voice unseen.

Moments later, another flash wand waived in the distance. "There you go, just follow that light and they'll take care of you."

He waved us on and motioned for the next car to move forward.

I drove over lawn toward the lights of our destination. Half way there, from the darkness, there appeared a woman, standing alone in the middle of the way.

Dressed in dark clothes, she was barely visible and I nearly hit her. I stopped just in time. My headlights illuminated her coat at hip level but her face was hidden in the darkness. I watched though the ashes scarring my windshield as she walked to the side of the car and stood, waiting.

I felt bad about nearly running her over but it was dark, I was tired and didn't feel a need to apologize. She'd been in the middle of the way in the dark. My stomach rumbled and bubbled again. I would have sold my soul for some Rolaids.

"Jeremy, she's trying to say something." Maggie whispered from the backseat.

I opened the window. She leaned in close and wheezed. Her thick, pungent breath filled the car with a smell so rancid it made me feel even more ill.

"I couldn't see you." I said, "You need to be careful, you're nearly invisible. Are you O.K.?"

I glanced sideways waiting for an answer. She was only a shadow in the dim light, dark and faceless under a large cowl of hair. I leaned back toward Richard when she finally spoke. Her voice was raspy and hard to define. She might have been twenty five or eighty, it was impossible to tell.

"What's the time you've got?" Her words rolled in on a wave of odor. I looked at the clock on the dashboard.

"Quarter to twelve." I said.

She pulled from the window and turned away. "Are you O.K.?" Maggie asked again.

"Fuck you!" she growled, then disappeared into the darkness.

"My God!" Richard rolled his window down to clear the air. "What the hell was that?"

"I have no idea." I replied.

"She smelled like death." Maggie said at last. "Let's get over there, this is too damn strange." I looked to her, then Richard. An odd chill shook me again, so I started forward to reach the safety of the lights.

Maggie whispered from the back, "Death affects people in different ways." A cold breeze wafted through the car, cleared the air and fed my chill so I closed all the windows and continued toward the trailer.

At the end we were met by one of the organizers who directed us to a parking spot. She called for someone to find

Thompson so I turned on the radio for a distraction while we waited.

Just after midnight the disc jockey warned people about trying to drive to the city. "State police report that highways are gridlocked for miles in both directions. The crowd is currently estimated at eight hundred thousand and growing." He suggested using Metro in the morning.

The announcer continued, "State police and emergency teams are unable to approach the Mall. The government plans a holiday tomorrow and requests those who aren't essential to stay home and watch coverage on TV "

Someone knocked on the window. I pushed the button to find a rather harried man with another clipboard and a small flashlight. He could have been a professor, tall and slender with graying hair and moustache. I imagined his demeanor was generally much calmer.

"Hi, Thompson here. They tell me you're the Donavans?"

Maggie leaned over my shoulder, "Yes, we are."

Tim looked in the car and back at his clipboard, "Says here that we were only expecting the two of you."

"I'm a 'Clay'." I explained, "We drove together."

"Clay…Clay." He turned a page, "I don't seem to find you

here. Clay, with a 'C'?"

"Yes, but I don't think I'm on your list."

"I'm sorry Mr. Clay, if you're not on the list then we don't have space for you." He looked up apologetically, "We don't even have room for those we're expecting. This thing has taken on a life of its own. It's getting out of hand" He shook his head and flashed a nervous smile.

"You're fortunate you arrived when you did." He looked past me to Richard. "We still have a bed left for the two of you, but I'm sorry there are no additional..."

"A bed?" Richard spoke loudly. "Maggie's my aunt. I don't think that'll work. When we arranged this on Wednesday, I informed..."

Maggie broke in, "I don't need a bed. I won't sleep tonight anyway. Richard, you take it."

"You're not a couple? I just thought..." Thompson stumbled. "We assumed..."

Richard broke in, "It's alright! Maggie, don't be silly," He spoke to Thompson, "If it's alright with you, Maggie can take the bed and we can sleep in the car." He continued "Maggie, I insist you get some rest. I don't care if you don't sleep. You need to take care of yourself."

Thompson looked at us, "I'm sorry, I'm really sorry. It's been absolutely chaotic here tonight. We have so much to do before tomorrow and time is running.

He looked back at his clipboard. "There's a briefing at six sharp tomorrow morning in the blue tent. Please be prompt. It's going to be a long busy day and it's imperative we have complete cooperation to make this work." He flipped through more papers, leafing back and forth,

"There's a press conference scheduled for eight. Reporters are everywhere and they'll probably hound you as soon as they're aware you're on site. Please don't make any official statements. They can be persistent. They all want a scoop. If they confront you, try to be civil. Most are on our side and the last thing we need is bad press. We've got some people to keep them at bay but we can't guarantee they won't get around us. Should you be approached, if at all possible, avoid saying anything before the press conference. Just give them a 'No comment'"

Someone shouted his name in the distance. He snapped to, and looked around. "Dammit!" He turned back to the window, "I'm sorry, I've got to run. If you need anything, you can ask the people wearing orange T-shirts." He pointed into the crowd, "They will do what they can to get what you need. Thank you in advance for your cooperation and patience."

He hurried off mumbling to himself.

The voice in the distance called again and he responded as he ran, "I'm here! Give me a second!" He looked back at us, then melted into the crowd.

"Looks like they could use some help." Maggie leaned forward and released her seat belt, "Can you let me out? I'll see if there's anything I can do."

Richard opened his door and stepped out. The seat back sprung forward and Maggie exited behind him.

He pleaded with her, "Please get some rest. We're all exhausted. We've got to be sharp tomorrow, for the family's sake. There are plenty of people who'll work all night. They'll do fine without you."

I stepped from the car to stretch my legs then climbed into the back seat, arched my back to cracking bones and settled in for the night.

Richard took Maggie by the arm. "I'll get some rest in the car if you promise to take the bed and use it."

She put her hand on his chest, "You were about to commit mayhem a while ago. You need to stop worrying about me, I'm fine, I can't fall any farther. I'm going to look over the area then

I'll find the bed."

Richard finally agreed with a hug. Maggie kissed him on the forehead, "I'll see you in the morning." With that she disappeared into the dark mass of wandering bodies.

SEVENTEEN

I floated weightless among clouds. When I leaned right, I slid through the air in that direction. When I leaned left, I did likewise. I was at peace and I wanted it to last forever.

In the distance were Richard and Maggie. They stood in a gentle summer field, adorned in sunlight. I leaned in their direction and moved silently toward them. Soft breezes caressed me, tossed my hair.

I drifted within a few yards until I could hear their conversation and floated silently above, unknown to them. I realized they were arguing vehemently. Everything was suddenly wrong. Richard screamed at Maggie, "I told you to rest, damn it! I meant rest!"

Maggie lost control and spat back an acrid sneer, "Rest? Rest? Is that all you can think of? Your wife and children are laying dead somewhere, burned cinders in the dust and you want me to rest!"

Richard's face grew red and bloated. Veins rose on his skin as he moved toward her and raised his hands to her throat.

I cried out but they couldn't hear me. I leaned toward them to move closer but lost balance and tumbled helplessly in the air.

Richard closed in and Maggie's sneer became even more pronounced. I had to stop them, end the madness, but try as I may, I couldn't do a thing but watch. The entire world became dark as the sun was swallowed in a cloud of amber dust and the field became a smoldering landscape of charred ash.

Richard screamed unintelligibly, his hands inches from her throat. Maggie arched her back and held her ground. There was something in her hand, gleaming, razor sharp. She bared her teeth in a sardonic grin.

Suddenly a voice came from behind me. It was cold and raspy and it laughed as Richard's fingers closed around Maggie's throat. It urged him on then demanded she strike as well. The voice screeched with demonic fervor.

I'd heard that voice, knew it in the darkest, most hideous reaches of my soul. It was somehow part of me but still, I was horrified. Realization washed over me in a shower of bloody sparks. My nerves twisted in agony. I tried to get away but hung helpless in midair. It was the voice of Death itself and it passed by within a breath. The stench was hideous. The nearer the specter came to them, the closer Richard and Maggie came to killing one another. The phantom laughed all the while, tormenting them, coaxing them on.

As a crippled hand reached to touch them, I gathered all my strength. It felt as if my soul would rupture and I forced a wrenching scream.

I sat straight in the back seat, gasping for air. It was barely daylight but people rushed toward us from all directions.

EIGHTEEN

"I understand you woke half the city this morning." Maggie said with a smile as we walked through morning fog. The air was chilled from a clear sky.

"Jeremy has nightmares." Richard said.

I put my hands in my pockets and walked behind, head down, sure everyone recognized me as the screamer.

Maggie led the way to the briefing. She wore a full length denim skirt and a bulky, dark green sweater. A flowered scarf adorned her head like a turban. She refused to hide her lack of hair so I assumed the scarf was for warmth on this brisk morning.

"Did you get any rest last night?" I finally asked.

"Enough." She smiled, "I seem to be doing better than you this morning."

Richard said, "I heard the Whitehouse tried to pull the plug on us last night, said there were too many people and not enough support. Conrad called it a safety issue. Evans refused. He claimed there'd be riots in the street if they tried to send people home at this point. He accused the President of obstruction and demanded that the American People be heard."

I glanced over, "I hate to agree with the President, but if things get out of hand with this many people, it could get real ugly. There's nowhere anyone can go."

"Apparently the National Guard will be joining us. The President demanded extra assistance since the Park Service and local police are completely overwhelmed."

Maggie looked around, "I don't think even the National Guard could help if this gets out of hand."

We found a series of food carts and got coffee. It was hot and welcomed in the damp morning air. I drained the cup and poured a refill.

It was just minutes before six o'clock so Richard and Maggie went off to their meeting. I stopped in a line at the portable toilets and overheard the conversation of a man who read from his phone, "They say a million and a half people are still on the roads not including those who are here. The entire District is closed down. We're here for the duration."

I found Richard and Maggie at the organizational tent. Thompson spoke to the collected speakers and participants one last time.

"Let's do our best to stay within the defined structure and keep things moving. We've got two hours of TV time and we want everyone to have their chance on the air."

As he spoke an assistant came to his side, whispered to him and handed him a paper.

"It's just been announced they've identified the uranium used at the Cape. It's part of the missing fuel from the St. Lucie plant in Southern Florida. That means it was locally sourced, folks. We now know where it came from, but not how they obtained it. Don't make any assertions around this information. We don't want to add to the tension. Let's allow the investigators do their job. If the crowd thinks someone in the US cooperated with the terrorists it might start a riot. Be careful that you talk only to the facts as we know them. Senator Evans will be able to gather forces after we complete this event in a peaceful manner."

He looked at his clipboard, brushed his hair back with his free hand and continued, "A few final notes; we're here for the duration. There's no way in or out, other than by air and the Pentagon is not about to remove security restrictions at this point in time. We're doing our best to cover medical situations as they arise and we're canvassing for health practitioners from the audience. There are just too many people. In the meantime, the National Guard has been brought on board."

The crowd began to mumble and Thompson raised his hand

get their attention, "Please! Please listen. This is important. Our security can't possibly deal with a crowd this size. The President requested the help and Senator Evans agreed. The Guard is here to assist. They are our safety net. Please respect them."

The group began to murmur again, People were becoming anxious, "Just one more important item. Can I have your attention? Please, just another moment."

They all quieted, "Last and most important, there are a lot of angry people out there. Inform them but don't incite them. It they become a mob they will be unstoppable. Be reasonable, be civil, be honest and be careful. If a hostile situation arises it will pose a real problem. Remember, we're at the eye of the storm if things come apart and there's no way out. I thank you in advance for your restraint."

He pulled a handkerchief from his back pocket and wiped his forehead, "If there are no more questions let's get started. The Press conference begins in forty minutes. A couple hundred reporters and several million people want to hear from us."

We left the briefing and Richard and Maggie examined the schedule while we made our way through the crowd.

My stomach became upset again. "I'll be back in a minute. I need to get rid of some coffee" I looked back as I walked off and watched them stroll together arm in arm.

As the distance grew I became filled with dread, lightheaded and apprehensive. I was suddenly overcome with the desire to run, to leave, just to get away. Even if I did run there was nowhere to go, there were just too many people. I took several deep breaths and tried to reduce the panic.

A short time later I wandered along, pushing and being pushed by waves of humanity. The path to the staging area was nearly impossible to navigate but as I approached, I saw a figure standing alone in the midst of the seething crowd; a woman with a cell phone in one hand and a cigarette in the other. I was instantly riveted. Although we were surrounded by the masses, they seemed to fade, leaving the two of us alone. She was spectacular, tall and slender, dressed in Levi's and a rust colored jacket that accented her auburn hair. I smiled.

Her face was tilted away from me as she spoke into her phone. Her left arm crossed her right and held the cigarette. She could have been an ad in a magazine.

I continued closer, drawn to her. When I was within a few feet she turned and saw me. "Jeremy!" She smiled, raised a finger, spoke a few final words, tapped the phone and slid it into her pocket. She inhaled from the cigarette, dropped it and crushed it beneath her boot as a stream of smoke preceded her words, "Jeremy, I'm so glad to see you."

She shook my hand and the morning mists disappeared.

"Kathryn," I said, "Damn, I can't believe I found you in this crowd. It's been a long couple days. How are you?"

"Great. I'm great. I take it you got Richard and Maggie here without incident? Is she doing alright? I've been worried about her with the stress and all."

I looked into her eyes as I nodded. It was great to see someone familiar in this craziness. I asked, "Why aren't you at the press tent?"

She laughed, "Jeremy, I've been writing the news, why would I want to ask about it?"

She said, "I'm planning to join Maggie and Richard later, after the event." She looked around, "doesn't look like we'll be able to get out of here for a while, but when we do, I've got access to a little place on the coast and I'll demand they step down for a while, take some time to unwind. I believe what they'll say today will kick some ass and start some fires. I want Maggie healthy as long as possible. After they make this appearance it'll be good to disappear for a while."

I realized I was still holding her hand when she squeezed

mine. I softened my grip and slowly let go. My heart was beating harder than it had in days.

Everyone else wants to focus on the President's responsibility and the possibility of some sort of corporate involvement. I'm still addressing the human losses with Maggie and Richard in the forefront. I want to present them as the bigger story, the families, the deaths and how all of it truly effects each of us. That's the part that usually gets left by the wayside. I've introduced them to the world, everyone knows who they are, what they've lost."

"But you've got to admit," I interrupted, "This has to be the granddaddy of all demonstrations. There's never been one bigger."

The silver in her eyes began to shine fire as she spoke, "Jeremy, it's not the demonstration. Sure, this is huge but only until the next politico gets caught with some sort of responsibility for some hideous carnage. There's sure to be even larger gatherings in time, but it all just continues."

Her passion increased. "The world will be moved by Richard and Maggie. People identify with them now and what they've lost. They represent our great failure. When the world sees the impact of this horror on their faces, when they hear it from real people, they'll be more prone stand up and change things. This may strike you as crass, but Maggie and I've discussed it at length. If we can get the country to know her, care for her, feel the loss when she passes on, her death might have a lasting impact. They'll see the effect on Richard and identify with more than the fleeting images of strangers they've become conditioned to on the evening news. We have the opportunity to make a major impression."

She was pacing now and pulled another cigarette from her breast pocket and a lighter from her Levi's. After a deep breath, smoke filtered toward me as she continued, "The world has grown to love Maggie, they identify with Richard's loss as their own. It will be true reality TV and hopefully, when she dies, it won't be just an acceptable loss."

"They've become known as a team so Richard's loss will continue to remind everyone of the pain. When Maggie's gone we'll all mourn her passing but we'll have Richard to carry us along. He'll become our conscience, our hope, our savior."

She pointed the cigarette at me and continued, "My point is, the moment all these people return to their homes, as soon as we find and punish the perpetrators everything will return to status quo. People forget too quickly. They need more than demonstrations. They need someone to identify with and hold their attention, someone to direct their feelings, to rise above all the mundane, political shit and actually move them."

I wondered at her enthusiasm, "So Richard's your leader and Maggie your martyr? Are you sure they want this? Does Richard understand what you have planned for him?"

"We've discussed and agreed on all the articles I've written. Together, we've decided the follow through when… you know," She dragged on her cigarette and released the smoke, "when Maggie's gone. Both of them want to have a greater impact. Something to give The Cape a lasting, universal imprint."

"I have plans. We've hashed out all the basic details and everything will be confirmed when we know how successful we've been today. There is also a huge force behind us to help make it happen."

She smiled, "I'd appreciate your input as well. Richard's your friend, I know you care about him and the last thing I want to do is add to his pain. If you're with us you can share your insight, I'd really like to hear your thoughts."

I looked into her eyes, "I believe you've got good intensions but I'd like know how they feel about this. If they're in agreement, I'll support you."

I took a breath, "I just don't want to see them hurt more.

They've already gone through far too much pain. If you swear you won't exploit them, I'll help any way I can. I'd do whatever it takes to stop things like this from ever happening again. "

She dropped her cigarette, ground it into the dirt, reached over and hugged me. I returned her embrace and held her tight.

NINETEEN

Helicopters created a torrent of swirling grass and maneuvered with difficulty to land in small clearings painstakingly carved from the masses. Guardsmen crawled from the bellies and took their places near the stage and on speaker platforms. Others made their way throughout the crowd.

Medical personnel joined the soldiers. The addition of hundreds more people added greatly to the claustrophobic atmosphere. An announcement welcomed the Guardsmen and assured everyone they were here to help.

The program started within minutes of noon, and as the crowd was welcomed to the largest single gathering of people on the earth, a cheer broke forth that was deafening.

Millions, as far as I could see, formed a patchwork of humanity. I was reminded of my first experience at the Grand Canyon, although I saw it, I couldn't quite comprehend the reality.

The cheering was frightening. Not so much the sound, as the feeling, the throbbing roar vibrated in my chest, in my soul. The force actually resonated in the ground as it spread from the center of the gathering and grew in a matter of minutes, until the entire city pulsed with applause.

Birds took flight and as the sound engulfed them. It was a power I'd never experienced before.

When at last there was silence again, the speakers began. They held the crowd in awe, brought people to tears and incited anger. Outbursts of applause and cheers slowed the progress, but not enough to create a problem. The orators masterfully led the audience. They controlled the energy like conductors with an orchestra.

Richard and Maggie conferred and prepared, with me as their gofer. I poured water, untangled cords and made myself useful in any sense I could.

Maggie had just finished her speech and Richard was escorting her back to her chair, when Senator Evans stepped to the microphone.

Suddenly there was a burst of noise. Hot, white flashes appeared in the right edge of my vision. Chips of wood leapt from the stage floor as though an invisible demon kicked splinters while it skipped across the platform. The Microphone stand was knocked down and the Senator followed, falling backwards, flailing his hands. The demon jumped along the row of chairs knocking everyone over in an instant. Richard stood next to me facing Maggie, his back to the crowd. He started to turn, then seemed to jump into Maggie's arms as they both crashed over chairs to the floor.

The demon danced just over my head, returned to center stage and proceeded it's destruction in the other direction. People on the far side tried to run but it was too swift. They whirled madly in all directions as their lives were torn from them.

I froze in panic and stood alone at center stage as the staccato pop, pop, pop, was replaced by a larger burst of sounds. Gunfire materialized from throughout the audience.

I watched as a man atop a large sound van was struck by gunfire, time and again. He collapsed and tumbled from the vehicle. One last flash was followed by a small pop. I looked down as I fell to my knees. My side burned with pain. The crowd boiled in panic. People charged in every direction with nowhere to go. Screams filled the city as more than a million people, shoulder to shoulder, tried in vain to escape.

I pushed the microphone stand up and used it to climb to my feet. The pain seared and when I clutched my side with both hands I nearly fell back down. I gazed across the mall at a sea of bodies as they writhed in waves of terror. People crushed one another, fleeing from the danger that no longer existed. The pain burned as I watched in shock. Something had to be done.

I tried to speak but nothing came out. Everything was wrong, desperately wrong. I trembled with fear. A mist seemed to cover my eyes. The world became unnaturally bright, as though the sun had intensified tenfold. I thought, My God, I'm dying.

I tried to talk again. A voice came at me from somewhere else as I whispered into the panic. Though it mimicked my words, it wasn't mine. Everything was suddenly soft and comfortably warm. Pain subsided as the voice and I spoke in unison. Fear melted and a sense of peace came over me.

"Stop!" The voice and I said softly. "Stop! It's over."

A few people stopped, looked up and stood motionless. It was as if they were frozen. Others began to notice, they too turned to stare. Within seconds, the hysteria ended as thousands upon thousands of eyes turned toward me, open wide with amazement.

"Stop!" The voice and I said together. I held my hands out to show those who couldn't hear, that the killing was done.

"Be calm, it's over." The voices assured us. "It's over now. We're all safe."

Eyes continued to stare. It almost seemed humorous. I smiled at them. A warmth flowed about me and I felt a harmony.

The voices had assured we were safe and all was well.

Suddenly flashes sparked from everywhere at the same time. I smiled as I turned to see them all, my hands still raised. They weren't the sharp white bursts of guns, but the warm yellow flashes from cameras. Everything began to soften and I reached for the microphone stand for support.

Someone grabbed me from behind. Others joined in and I rose into the air. I was floating again, as in the dream. No effort, no care. This time, instead of a warm summer field below, I was surrounded by faces, by calm smiling faces. And from everywhere came hands. Hands touching me, gently caressing me.

"Why are they touching me?"

TWENTY

I awoke on the floor of an ancient forest where trees reached to the sky. The darkness was terrifying and I waited for my eyes to adjust to the pale light, listening for any evidence of wild animals that might see me as a meal. There was nothing but a vast stillness broken only by the wind through branches a hundred feet above.

As I tried to figure my bearings, what was north, what might be south, I noticed a faint glow in the distance toward the peak of a mountain. I needed to reach that glow; it seemed my only hope of rescue.

I made my way through dense underbrush, vines fought me and brambles tore at my clothing. The way was steep and extremely difficult but I had to move toward the light. I had to escape this hopeless isolation.

I followed an indistinct path through the forest until I came to a dead end. There was no way to continue. I retraced my steps to a spot where I could try a different direction, and continued to climb upward toward the light.

After a time I fell to the forest floor, exhausted. The damp pine needles were cool against my face and I rested. Thirst grew and I wished for a river, a stream, a patch of snow. There was only the damp earthiness of the forest, nothing to drink, or eat. I had to continue on to survive. The light was my only hope.

I stumbled forward, crawling through thickets that scratched my skin. The way became even steeper and the air thinned. Several times I wanted to stop, to give up, but I had to go on, there was no choice.

I continued higher and still higher until I could hardly draw a breath. My legs cramped but I had to push onward, upward.

As I neared the peak, the glow intensified and I found determination to push on. I crested a hilltop and froze with horror. The glow that I had spent my energy climbing toward was a huge forest fire.

Flames engulfed trees as far as I could see. They consumed everything in front of me to the horizon. My salvation had become a funeral pyre.

The fire was fueled by air and all the oxygen from my lungs was sucked out, dissipated in the heat of the raging inferno.

There was no retreat, no escape. I closed my eyes, lay down, and curled into a ball to wait for the fire to cremate me.

The heat's intensity grew and when I could no longer endure, there was a huge popping sound and the temperature subsided.

I lay there, awaiting death, but nothing seemed to happen. The raging flames were silent. The heat of the pyre was gone. I heard only wind through ancient branches.

I opened my eyes to darkness and thought I was surrounded by forest again. As I examined the murky situation, I realized I was in the vast shadow of a cemetery with winds whipping through limitless gravestones; both ancient and new, huge memorials and insignificant plaques.

I walked among endless paths bordered by the dead. Stones displayed names of everyone I'd ever known; everyone I'd ever loved. They were all dead but me. I alone survived in this world.

I was overcome with terror. I panicked, turned and started to run blindly down the mountainside. I ran through the ashes of what had been. I ran into underbrush that still was and I continued down.

I burst through a thicket and found myself at the edge of a cliff. I tried to stop but momentum carried me into the air.

I fell. The bed bounced as I grabbed sheets to stop the dissent. The sound of my pounding heart rasped in my ears and seemed to echo in the darkness. I was drenched with sweat.

TWENTY ONE

I found myself in a heavy, drug induced fog and faintly remembered dreams, but they were distant and hazy. I looked around and recognized nothing. The light was unnaturally green from old florescent bulbs.

Misty voices came from somewhere. I raised my head to find two people standing near the foot of the bed, backs to me. I couldn't tell who they were. I tried to speak but my mouth was cotton. "Excuse me, "came as a whisper that even I couldn't hear. I cleared my throat. It was sandpaper on stone and nearly closed. I needed water desperately.

"This is it!" She said. "Here comes the part I was talking about."

I tried to speak once more and something finally came. "Hey! Where am I?"

They didn't hear me. I looked around for someone else who might help. When I raised up a pain tore at my side. I grunted loudly as I fell back to the bed. The noise finally drew attention.

They turned and looked at me with surprise. The woman's green eyes were on fire. There was a look of raw power on her face. She was hazy, outlined in a warm glow. Something stirred inside of me as I tried to focus. She seemed comfortably familiar.

"My God, you're awake. Quick," she rushed forward to me, "look!" She pointed to a television suspended from the ceiling.

There, on the screen, was this same woman. It came upon me like the summer sun; it was Kathryn, Kathryn Lawson. Here as well as on the TV. Her recorded image interviewed an elderly woman who was visibly excited.

"...that's when we stopped. We all thought we were dead. People were pushin' and tryin' to get away. Guns were going off everywhere. That's when it happened. Some man was pushin' me, about to knock me down. All of a sudden he freezes and says, 'Oh my God!' I turned to see what he was lookin' at and there he was, up on the stage. He's got blood on his side and blood on his hands and his hands up in the air. He whispered that we were all saved. It was OK and we could calm down. And everybody did. It was a miracle. Everybody just stopped, all at the same time."

"Can you tell us anything more?"

"Yes," she paused, "Yes I can." The camera moved in for a close-up. "People might think I'm crazy, but I saw it." She became very serious, raised her eyebrows and said in little more than a whisper, "The man had a halo around him. That's why everyone stopped. He was surrounded by a halo! It could have been Jesus, down from the cross standin' there. Everyone saw it. He had a halo!"

The scene changed to a studio and a news man continued.

"And here again, is the footage from the disaster in Washington yesterday." Video cameras were focused on the Senator when he suddenly disappeared. There was great confusion as the camera operator tried in vain to follow the action. He finally turned to a guardsman who was desperately looking around for the sniper. When the soldier finally made visual contact, the camera swung wildly through the crowd of shocked faces. All the while, the sounds of gunshots rang from the TV speaker.

It was difficult to catch a breath. Thoughts and memories flooded in, mixing and churning together as I tried to sort them. What was reality? Which were the dreams? Oh God! Maybe it wasn't a dream after all.

The camera stopped panning just in time to see a figure fall from the top of a van. Then came pandemonium, screaming and total panic. The crowd pushed and clawed their way in every direction. The cameraman tried to continue recording. He held the camera in the air, apparently to leave a record of his demise.

He was knocked to the ground and still the camera kept recording.

Kicking feet, legs and screams of frightened people filled the scene. The confusion was terrifying. Tears began to pour from my eyes. Not for my experience, but for the cameraman who would soon die on national television.

Then, as quickly as it began, the panic ended. People stopped kicking, stopped pushing. The screams and hysteria subsided. The camera rose, swinging wildly from the ground, to people, to sky and back again. Finally, the scene swung once more toward the stage. The picture focused and there, in front of me, filling the screen, was a man the woman had spoken of.

There, surrounded by a radiant glow, stood the man who could have been Jesus. He faced the millions of people, and now the world, bloodied hands outstretched, in complete tranquility. My head began to throb and I felt I might vomit when I realized, it was me.

The announcer spoke over a freeze frame, "A miracle? The Messiah? We will explore more information about Jeremy Clay after these few words."

"Turn it off! " The voice was a high panicked whisper and I would have laughed if it hadn't come from me. "Turn it off!" I demanded. "What the hell is this?"

Kathryn sat at my side as the man turned the set off. "It's alright Jeremy relax. It's all going to be OK." She reached across me and pushed a button on a small control. The terror of what I'd just heard remained.

The man moved toward the door without a word. I saw him for the first time. He was tall and slender in a dark suit. His hair was thick, bushy brown sprinkled with grey.

"Who is that?" I might have known him but I couldn't tell. He glanced back at me just before he opened the door to leave. He had an almost indiscernible smile. A chill traced my spine as he nodded stoically and disappeared into the hallway.

In the next moment, a nurse rushed into the room and ushered Kathryn out.

"Mr. Clay, I'm happy to see you're awake. I want you to know that you're getting the best care available. You'll stay here with us for a few days and soon you'll be good as new."

She checked a monitor next to the bed and smiled a rather unconcerned smile. "Your doctor will be here in just a few minutes to talk with you. You can relax now, Mr. Clay. The worst is behind you."

The door opened and a man in a white jacket stood with his

back to me, talking to a group of people just outside. Kathryn was in the crowd along with the man who had been in my room. The doctor quickly glanced over his shoulder at me, turned back to someone outside, and shook his head. Finally, he entered, but half way across the room he stopped and looked back.

A second man, dressed in a dark blue suit, spoke for moment with Kathryn and her friend. He nodded to them then joined the doctor, closing the door behind him.

TWENTY TWO

The doctor seemed preoccupied, unconsciously adjusting the small collar of his lab coat again and again. He glanced uncomfortably toward the man in blue as he spoke, "Mr. Clay, I'm Doctor Sanford. You are at Inova hospital in Alexandria. You were transported here yesterday, after being wounded. Do you remember anything about the incident?"

I stared back in silence. His look was stoic and he spoke as though the news was bad. I braced for the worst.

"You were struck by a single bullet." He paused and then continued as he read from a clipboard, "It entered just beneath the lower left rib, and exited through the back. The angle was fortunate, the wound clean and the bullet didn't damage any organs. You're an extremely lucky man."

He looked to me, quickly glanced at the man in blue, and back. I watched his eyes for what felt like an eternity and tried to muster the courage to ask about the others. He must have anticipated my questions and continued.

"I'm sorry, Mr. Clay. You were the only survivor. The others on the stage were all pronounced dead at the scene."

I fell back into my pillow. "All of them? Everyone?"

He turned and faced the TV, "Everyone on the stage died," his voice fell off a bit as he looked over his shoulder, "everyone but you."

"Your wound would have been fatal if the path of the bullet had entered at a slightly different angle. It was a miracle you lived."

Visions of Richard lying dead filled my thoughts. I started to weep. "Why!"

He bent down and placed his hand on my wrist. He looked at his watch, "Mr. Clay, this is agent Fulton, from the FBI. He's in charge of the investigation. If you feel up to it he has more information and a few questions."

Fulton stepped to my side and nodded, "Mr. Clay, Agent Fulton, David. We're happy to see you're still with us."

He was too clean cut, too proper. I didn't like the man the moment I saw him. I certainly wasn't ready to talk about anything. For God's sake, my best friend was dead. I needed time. I turned my head and closed my eyes.

He continued, "There were no other survivors on the stage. The gunman was a disturbed individual from Mississippi named Klein," He looked in a notebook, "Orville Klein. He's well known to the Bureau. We have an extensive file on him. I know this is difficult Sir, but have you ever heard of him? Was there any reference to Orville Klein in any of the meetings? Any mention of a direct or implied threat made to your people by anyone the past couple days?"

I shook my head no.

"Kline had threatened Senator Evens on Facebook several times. He claimed the man was persecuting the President. There were letters as well, written to the Senator. Even though we have that information, we're looking for any possible relationships with the others who died. Although the shooting began as soon as Senator Evans took the stage, which suggests he was the target, we can't discount the fact that it might be otherwise. We have to investigate every possibility.

I heard myself shouting through the fog, "You knew this man? You had files on him and still allowed him to bring a gun to Washington and kill all those people? A Senator for God's sake! What the hell…" The doctor pushed the button on a remote next to me and I instantly felt my arm warm and the room became more indistinct.

I heard the agent through a hollow echo, "If you can remember anything, even if it seems minor or irrelevant, please forward the information. Shock can conceal critical memories and often, details seem unimportant. If anything unusual comes to mind, please pass it on. Don't worry about how irrelevant it might seem, anything could help our investigation." He placed a business card on the table.

I closed my eyes, "No more. Please. No more. I just want to wake up," but this time, there was no dream to escape from.

Someone else spoke, "He'll sleep now. He needs rest."

Within moments the room faded. Warmth and darkness surrounded me.

TWENTY THREE

I opened my eyes and seemed engulfed in a mist, my ears hissed and the throbbing in my head made me forget where I was. Several minutes passed before I remembered why I was here. Fading sleep was quickly edged out by a growing remorse. I was terrified and immensely alone. I wanted to run but could barely move; besides I had nowhere to go. Emptiness overwhelmed me, I started to hyperventilate. My ribcage ached all the more.

"Dear God, why me? Why the hell did you leave me here?" My fists slammed the bed and met no resistance. I pulled the pillow over my face and screamed until my throat became raw and I was exhausted, barely able to move. The waves of frustration receded for a moment until I caught a breath and they came crashing in again and hit me with full fury.

I finally collapsed, but the emptiness grew and expanded. Under the pillow I was hopelessly alone with no reason to go on.

"Save the world!" I thought, "For what? So some crazy asshole can butcher everyone anyway? So we can live in constant pain?" The wave hit me again and I was overcome once more. Death was no longer my enemy. I was ready. I welcomed it.

Time lost all meaning. Depression washed over me again and again until I decided it was best to go the way of my friends. There was no reason to continue. I began to plan my demise.

The door opened and I inadvertently jumped. Someone had intruded to postpone my fate. The last thing I wanted was company. I glared at the nurse who entered as she spoke. "Mr. Clay! You're awake! How are you feeling?"

I didn't answer. I stared at the ceiling and mustered all my strength to retain some dignity. I was exhausted and in considerable pain but I lay in silence.

She came to my side. "You look uncomfortable. Here. If the pain gets too intense just press this button. She picked up the remote and showed me how to use it.

I hesitated, but at her coaxing, I pushed the button. Anything to get her to leave so I could attend to my plan.

She knelt near me and looked deeply into my eyes, "You know," she said at last, "I really wanted to be there Saturday. I had to work till eight that morning. There wasn't any point in even trying by then."

She leaned close. There were tears in her eyes. "I've got two kids and I'd really like to see them grow up without all these wars and murders. I just want to tell you how much I appreciate what you've done and how sorry I am that things turned out the way they did."

The pain began to subside ever so slightly. She brushed her hand across her eyes, bent down, gently hugged me and whispered softly in my ear, "I believe in you."

Tension tightened my muscles to stone. She pulled away without looking, took her tray and rushed from the room.

I was alone again. I pulled the pillow over my face to devise my end.

TWENTY FOUR

"Mr. Clay, how are we this afternoon?" The doctor came over and stood by my side.

"I'd be better if I could have visitors other than you people."

He smiled awkwardly, "Because of the situation and concern for your wellbeing, they want you to remain inaccessible for safety sake."

"My phone, where is my phone, at least I could talk to someone."

He shook his head, "I'm afraid this wing is rather isolated and secured so cell phones don't function here. In the meantime, I need to check your dressings and see how you're wound is coming along."

He asked a few questions as he surveyed my stitches. "You seem to be healing very nicely. I'd like to think I've had a small hand in that." He looked at me with a smile in his eyes.

His expression changed to one more serious. The smile was gone as he spoke, "The hospital chaplain would like to speak with you Mr. Clay. It's a service for trauma patients. It's your choice if you feel up to it. I know it would mean a lot to him. Can I bring him in?"

Thoughts of suicide had passed but loneliness still prevailed. I was almost ready to share my pain. "I suppose, when could he come?"

"He's here right now if that's OK?" I nodded and lay back as the doctors footsteps moved away. The door closed with a sigh as he left the room.

A moment later it opened again. The chaplain entered but stopped just inside the room.

"Mr. Clay? I'm Chaplain Moralez. How are you, today?" He sounded nervous, a choppy voice, like a boy calling on his first date. He looked like he hadn't yet graduated high school, seemed far too young to be a minister. He had nearly black hair, olive skin and the slightest hint of an accent.

I nodded to him. "Please, come in Chaplain."

He approached my bed, "Mr. Clay, I'm here to help should you want to talk about your experiences on Saturday. I would like to be your friend."

As he spoke, his expression changed from that of a 'friend', to one of a scientist looking through a microscope. He was extremely distant, as though something overwhelming were on his mind. We studied one another in silence for several painful seconds.

I couldn't take any more and broke the stillness. "Thank you for seeing me, Chaplain. I truly appreciate your time. I really need to talk with somebody that's not here to drug me."

The intensity of his gaze increased as though he tried to look inside me. He apparently hadn't heard a word I'd said. He studied something much deeper. My anxiety grew and emptiness chiseled through the drug haze. Fear welled up as this holy man searched for something unknown.

At last he spoke. It came softly, guarded, and planned, "Mr. Clay, I've seen the films. I've heard the statements. Being here with you, I almost feel something...Almost. However..."

His words fell off. He took a breath and continued, eyes wide and glazed, "I can't endorse what happened as a miracle. I just can't in good faith say that the church will support you in your quest. I'm very sorry."

He became fidgety and searched for words to end our conversation. I shook my head slowly trying to understand what he was talking about. I looked at him with growing fear and confusion. I just wanted him to leave.

He continued staring directly into my eyes and then turned his gaze to the wall. "You look tired." he said at last. "I'll let you rest."

He made an audible gulp as he swallowed, "If there is anything more I can do for you, please feel free to call for me. I'm here to help. Remember, the church offers an avenue for you to sort things out."

With that, he rushed to the door. As he sealed the room behind him, I tried to figure out what had just happened. The doctor said the Chaplin would offer relief, but he'd left me in deeper distress. I pushed the button on the remote, closed my eyes and prayed the drugs would kick in, but the mystery of his words burrowed through me. Finally, drugs and exhaustion won over and I faded into oblivion.

TWENTY FIVE

A sharp knock at the door fractured the boredom. Kathryn entered with a huge smile and an armful of newspapers. She came to my side and threw them on top of me. I cringed from the impact.

"Oh my God! I'm so sorry!" She reached down and grabbed the bundle. Papers fell across the floor.

I couldn't believe she had brought more news of the murders. "I really don't want to see this." I turned my head and waved her away.

"No Jeremy," her smile became concern. "It's not what you think. You don't remember, do you?"

"Remember what? What the Hell is going on? Am I crazy? I have no idea what everyone is talking about?" I almost shouted, "I've become a captive audience for every irrational person who happens by this room."

"I'm sorry," she said and she shook her head. "I honestly thought you'd remember. I truly thought you knew."

Excitement began to build in her eyes as she spoke. "Let me find…" She pulled the top newspaper, glanced at it and put it aside. She searched through a few that had fallen on the floor until she found one. "Here, this is in English." She handed the paper to me.

"What...?" I opened it cautiously and examined the front page. There, covering the top half was a photo of me on the stage in DC. I swallowed heavily. My bloodied hands were raised in the air. My expression embodied unconditional peace. An odd glow surrounded me.

"What the hell?"

"Read it!" She coaxed, "Read the caption."

I tried to read but my eyes were continually drawn back to the picture. I began to tremble as the significance rushed in. It was absurd. There in bold print, under *my* photo were the words;

"THE NEW MESSIAH"

A soft buzz filled my ears, the room started to sparkle as my vision faded. When the lights dimmed there was nothing to do but lay back and wait for the inevitable.

Through the darkness I heard, "Jeremy!" The words filtered faintly through the hum in my head.

"Jeremy, wake up!" Light started to brighten through a small fissure that opened to the room. It slowly expanded and a soft pat on my face brought it closer.

"Are you all right?" A few more pats and I saw Kathryn, calling me back.

"That's right", I thought, "its Kathryn. Kathryn's here."

"Are you all right?" she asked again.

I shook my head and the world slowly returned.

"Are you all right?" she demanded, "For God's sake, answer me!"

I suddenly remembered. Her frightened eyes were riveted on me. I remembered the paper, it lay on my chest. I took another from the few left on the bed and opened it with shaky hands. There, under my picture, written in some foreign script was the word, "JESUS"

She shared five others with me, my photo covered the front page of each of them.

"What have you done?" I found another English version and scanned the story.

> During the massacre, a man stood in the midst of a hail of bullets while a heavenly glow emanated from him. He was untouched by the destruction that slaughtered eleven others on the stage surrounding him.

He raised his hands, offered a few soft words, and the terrified masses stopped as if by a miracle. The horror ended in an instant. This single man prevented certain death to thousands.
He called for peace and calm where chaos reigned, and it instantly came to pass. Not a single person was injured. Several witnesses believed they were visited by divine presence. The entire world now debates the significance of the event and whether the man actually performed a heavenly act. The question on everyone's mind remains, might this be the return of the Chosen One? Are we witnessing the Messiah?"

I couldn't think. If words could even express what I felt, none would come. I stared at the paper in disbelief.

Kathryn sat next to me on the bed, put her arms around me and pulled me close. I tried to move and realized how weak I actually was. While we sat in silence, her manner changed dramatically.

After several moments, she suggested, "Would you like to discuss the situation again? I don't mean to push you too quickly. I thought you'd be pleased. What do you say? Are you ready?"

I eased back onto the bed and closed my eyes. I was now convinced I'd gone thoroughly mad. Maybe it was a reaction to the drugs, possibly another nightmare gone wild. I tried to assure myself I would wake up. I was even willing to open my eyes and find Ellen lying next to me.

I said nothing as I waited for reality to return and rescue me from some practical joke. A laugh came from somewhere deep inside. Kathryn shifted, apparently uncomfortable with my reaction.

I felt the warmth of her hand on my stomach and the situation struck me hard. When she shifted I reached for her so she wouldn't leave. Instead, I looked to see her lean over to pull her phone from her purse.

"I want you to hear this again. It might explain a little."

She tapped the screen several times until she found what she was searching for, "I recorded this when we talked that morning."

She ran her finger over the screen and my voice came from a speaker. "I swear, I'll help you any way I can. I'd do whatever it takes to stop things like this from ever happening again."

Her eyes were wide. "Jeremy, you said you wanted to help. The situation was there and the timing was perfect. If I'd had the opportunity to discuss it with you I certainly would have. We have the chance of a lifetime. You'd already agreed to help, I couldn't let something this important fade!"

Confusion erupted into anger, though I could hardly speak I

shouted, "I agreed to help Richard and Maggie. I never said I'd pose as Jesus! How the hell do you expect me to do something like this? I'm lying here, helpless in some hospital, for God's sake, and you're telling everyone I walk on water? I'll be destroyed. I won't even be able to show my face. Kathryn, I said I'd help, but this is insane!"

She closed her eyes and drew a deep breath. "I'm sorry if you feel you've been used. But if you'll let me explain…." Her request was tender, beguiling. I sighed heavily, clenched my teeth, and held my breath.

She spoke softly with conviction. "First, and you've got to believe me, I didn't create this. I had absolutely nothing to do with what people believe they saw. It grew from the terror surrounding the situation. They grasped at any explanation that could help them understand the disaster. Fox interviewed the woman and broadcast what she said, live."

She took a breath, "Whether those around her actually believed as she did or agreed with her just to get on TV, we'll never know. The reporter went along with it and led them on. When word spread, all the networks followed the same theme and the story took on a life of its own."

Her hands began to move wildly as she spoke. She took a

pack of cigarettes from her coat pocket and continued, waving the pack in front of her, "The woman thought she was about to die. She said she prayed to Jesus and the crowd suddenly stopped. She looked up and saw you. She thought you answered her prayers."

"People around her began to agree. The story spread like a gasoline fire. Nearly everyone claimed to believe you were divinely inspired."

She stopped to take a cigarette from the pack, held it between her fingers and went on, "In most cases, something this crazy would be laughed off before the six o'clock news. But all the agencies jumped on the bandwagon for position and it covered the globe within an hour. They all fanned the flames for headlines and it grew so quickly, no one could stop it even if they wanted. "

She put the cigarette between her lips, took out a lighter and squeezed it till a flame appeared. Then stopped, looked around, and put the lighter away. She smiled at me and removed the cigarette.

"The entire world saw the film before anyone could question it and Fox certainly wasn't about to abandon their advantage." She sat on the edge of the bed, "Jeremy, no one manufactured what those people saw or felt. Honestly, something extraordinary did happen. I had absolutely nothing to do with that."

She hesitated, "But things started to get out of hand, everyone wanted to touch you, the networks wanted to own you. I called in a favor and my contact agreed to get you to safety. You were carried to a Guard copter and we brought you here. Virtually no one knows where you are. The broadcasters are going crazy trying to identify your whereabouts. You're a mystery, the Savior who's disappeared.

"As your associate and with the authority of my contact, I was given responsibility and took over the situation. I truly think you should stay hidden for a while, at least until you're well. In the meantime I'll attempt to keep the hounds at bay and the story moving in the correct direction. "

I tried to sit up but pain stabbed through me. I stopped, leaned on one elbow, "What the hell am I supposed to do now! I'm not a damned Messiah, hell, the only time I've been inside a church was at Richard's wedding."

I pleaded, "Kathryn, you've got to get me out of here. You can't believe the people who keep coming in this room. If this is what I've got to look forward to…"

"Jeremy, relax. The staff is all military and under strict guidelines. They can't release any information. You need to be here a while to heal. In the meantime we'll have the details all worked out about what will happen when you're released. This is going to be wonderful. It's what we all wanted. And who knows, it just might have been some act of God. It could have a purpose larger than we can imagine."

She picked up another paper, "We're studying all possible implications as well as possibilities. Seriously, I watched the entire event over and over, and for the life of me, I can't even begin to explain it. Some of those people believe in their hearts they experienced a Holy presence. When a solitary woman raised the idea, it became universal in a matter of hours. It's beyond comprehension."

My breath was heavy, the room spun and I collapsed back on the bed.

"Jeremy, you've got to admit, it was pretty damned extraordinary. That son of a bitch shot everyone on the stage with an assault rifle and you were the only one who survived. That in itself is explainable but when thousands of people panicked, you whispered a few words and they all stopped. How do you account for that?"

I couldn't begin to answer her. I just wanted to scream, to end it all and disappear.

She threw the unlit cigarette in the trash can, "Listen, I've done this for nearly a dozen years. I've seen all the lies, the indignation, the promise of change."

She began to pace and pulled another cigarette from the pack. "We hoped all the wars would finally bring peace, open our eyes. Last Christmas the biggest selling gifts were guns and war games. Kids wear camos to school each day. More of them than you can imagine plan killing sprees. They sit in front of video games and learn how to get the greatest body count for the most points."

"Television has nothing but carnage on the evening news. It's entertainment now. Dead bodies in mass graves, suicide bombers, our enemies hanging in warehouses and beheadings on the web. They've broadcast death every night until it's become acceptable. We anonymously kill our enemies and at the same time sell them weapons to kill each other and use against us. Everyone acts like killing one another is the only goddamned way to make a buck."

She was moving faster now, a lioness in a cage, determined, not angry, "This country's become feared globally. We've built the most devastating arsenals in the history of the world and we market them to everyone. For what? So others can protect themselves from us. Can you even imagine how threatened the rest of the world must feel? They're attacking us for God's sake and when one of our weapons is used against us, we're fucking shocked. A few short months later and Washington wants us to move on. The president tells us to put it all aside and live like nothing's happened and all the while they scare the hell out of everyone with fear of another disaster so they can keep selling war."

She looked at the new cigarette, crumbled it and threw it in the trash with the last. "Some of the most articulate and vocal people in the country were brought together to stop the cycle. Now, most of them are gone.

"Four days ago, headlines spoke of taking back our nation. Three days ago the news reported millions of people clogging the capitol and called them activists and anarchists. The purpose behind the rally was secondary and confined to the middle of the local section. Had it been just a rally, the following day would have seen nothing but complaints about the costs to taxpayers for the cleanup and fluff pieces about babies that were born. It would have been a battle to get the reasons even mentioned in the back of the entertainment section."

She came back to the bed and kneeled beside me, "Even with the shootings, the purpose of the Evans investigation would have become secondary to the murders. We'd see reports about people with mental problems, drugs and arguments about gun control again. By this time it all would have become old news and some actor's marriage or divorce would have taken page one."

The silver sparks in her eyes seemed to melt into soft radiant green, "My point is, everything we've strived for, the reason all those good people died would be gone, forgotten! There would be a few follow up bios to tie up loose ends. Everything would have faded away. Opposition leaders are gone. Homeland would argue national security as the rationale to prevent another demonstration. After all, terrorists are gone, Klein is dead, the nation is safe again."

She felt for her cigarette pack, "Momentum's been terminated, Jeremy. Evans is dead and congress is stepping softly while the president screams, 'I told you so.' People throughout the country are afraid and being bullied, but now you can turn it all around."

"Why me?" I clenched my eyes again. "Why the hell does it have to be me?"

Kathryn took my hand. "I don't know why, why you lived when no one else did. I'm truly happy it was you. I realize it's difficult to accept, but believe me, it'll most likely last only a few months. People trust in you, they need to have some peace right now. If we do this properly, we just might be able to make some real changes in this country, in this world. At the very least, you'll influence others to pick up the torch."

Her voice softened but silver began to sparkle in her eyes again, "If we work things properly we might be able to stretch this into a year. Imagine what an entire year of worldwide media could accomplish. Do you have the slightest concept what you could do? The power you'll have to right things?"

She dropped my hand and flailed hers with excitement, "This opportunity has never existed before. You've been offered a gift, an ultimate gift. For God's sake, Jeremy, we can't even consider letting this pass."

"Kathryn," I sounded like a pleading child, "This is too much. I can't...I just..." The medication and tension were taking their toll. "I don't know. I need time. I need rest."

I had nothing left, no fight, no energy, my thoughts were in tangles. The bed moved and a gentle kiss graced my forehead. I slid softly into sleep and all was gone.

TWENTY SIX

The sand was warm on the bluff overlooking the ocean. In the distance a family played in the surf. A man carried a toddler on his shoulders, a woman held an older girl's hand. They ran back and forth, slipped into the waves and returned to the shore. I heard their laughter and felt their delight.

I found myself laughing with them. Their love drifted to me on the wind. It was warm and familiar. I wanted so much to be part of their joy that I plodded through the sand to where they played. The sounds intensified as I approached.

As I neared, the children noticed me and shouted my name. The girl jumped up and down then ran my way, squealing with excitement. The man put the young boy in the sand, took his hand and walked after his daughter.

The woman called too. It wasn't until I got closer that I realized it was Donna. The love I'd felt at a distance washed over me like a tidal wave and I broke into a run.

When Heather and I closed on one another, I scooped her up. I didn't miss a step as I ran to Donna with her daughter in my arms.

I put the girl down and reached for her mother. When we hugged, warmth and tranquility filled the void I'd known for months.

I told her how much I missed them, how lost I'd been since they were gone. As I explained, the peace was shattered by the sounds of gunfire. I pushed Donna to the ground and looked for Richard.

A moan tore from my throat. He lay in the sand, bleeding. I broke and ran to him. Heather clutched her mother. I passed Tyler who sat in the sand screaming.

When I reached Richard he was no longer on the beach, instead he was on the stage in Washington DC. I knelt beside him and he reached for me. Blood was everywhere. He spoke in a whisper so I dragged him into my lap and leaned close to hear.

"Richard why? Tell me why?" I sobbed convulsively as his warm blood drenched my slacks.

A hand touched my shoulder. Donna stood beside me, smiling gently. The children came close and hugged me. A warm breeze mussed my hair.

Richard spoke, "Jeremy. It's alright." I looked down, shocked to find the blood stains gone. He rolled from my lap, stood and pulled me up beside him. His wounds had vanished and he was alive. He took me by the shoulders, looked in my eyes and smiled, "We died for you. Don't ever forget that."

A light appeared so bright it burned. One nurse held me against the bed while another injected something into my IV. A choking, guttural wail filled the room as I thrashed against the body that forced me down. Slowly, I remembered where I was. Within seconds numbness climbed my arm. I tried to speak to the horrified faces when all my thoughts ceased.

TWENTY SEVEN

I awoke in darkness. There was movement in the hallway, the quiet bustle of the hospital starting a new day. This was Wednesday, as close as I could figure. Three days of near solitude. The dream of the previous night re-ran once more in my thoughts. I shook violently to try and erase it. My stomach throbbed in reply, I couldn't release the scene; Richard staring into my eyes, "We died for you!"

I reached for the call button and pressed it several times. I wanted someone from this world to talk to. I needed to know that I was still capable of rational conversation. I was truly beginning to doubt my sanity.

Minutes later, after squeezing the button several more times, a nurse entered the room and turned on the light. "Are we doing better this morning?" She looked exhausted but smiled and spoke in her best bedside manner. She checked the chart and gazed over the notes, "You had a rough night but it looks like you'll be fine. What can I get for you?"

She was young, maybe twenty three but the lines in her smile said she could have been a much older woman or someone who'd had more than a long night. She was patient. She waited for me to explain why I'd nearly strangled the call button.

My thoughts were glazed. I couldn't very well tell her I'd insisted on attention because of a dream. I could almost hear my plea, "I'm really not a lunatic, I'm God. You've got me isolated in this hospital for my protection, but actually all my friends died for me, because, you see, I'm God!"

Every thought sounded ludicrous, so I remained silent. She stepped next to the bed, placed her hand on my shoulder and spoke in a near whisper, "Something was bothering you. Sure you don't want to talk about it?"

Aside from Kathryn, this was the first physical contact I'd had in three days that wasn't meant to sedate me, wrestle me into restraints or change an IV. Her only purpose was to sooth me, to ease my fear. I took her hand and held it next to me. Her eyes widened and the lines on her face softened. She gazed as though she'd discovered an old friend in a hostile crowd.

"I'm sorry." I said at last, "I hope I didn't drag you away from something important. I just woke up after a really bad night. I'm O.K. now."

She squeezed my shoulder and her smile was more than bedside manner.

As I looked into her eyes, everything poured forth and try as I may, I couldn't stop myself, "You can't believe what I've been through these last months. Nearly everyone I know is dead. I'm the only one left, and everyone who comes in here wants something from me. They want my blood, they want my life, they want me to be part of some damn sideshow. I need someone who doesn't want to study me or use me. I need to…"

Panic rose in my voice so I stopped, swallowed and took a breath. "I need somebody, that's all. I just need someone."

The smile faded and lines appeared again, "It's hard, I know. I truly know how difficult it can be." Her trained manners returned, "Give it a while and know that time heals. It's true, I've seen it happen more often than I'd like."

Her thoughts seemed to wander as she spoke. She wasn't talking to me any longer. "Sometimes waiting is the most difficult thing we have to do. It seems like the pain will never end, never get better, like everything is crashing in around us all at once."

She wasn't reciting any longer. The words came from her heart and whatever instigated them was agonizing. Anguish overcame her features, I squeezed her hand to bring her back.

She focused a bit and looked at me, surprised, "I'm sorry, I'm supposed to be here to help you."

She hesitated, then stuttered, "Thank you so very much."

I was confused, why did she thank me?

"Let's see what we can do to help." She stood and looked around my bed. "Where in the world is that phone? Maybe you can call someone. Is there a friend you can talk with?" She disappeared under my bed. "Here we go. What's it doing back here?" She pulled the set out and placed it beside me. The receiver fell off and I heard dial tone.

"Sounds like it's working. They must have put it out of the way last night." She hung up the receiver and smiled, "Sometimes, if you just talk with a friend it seems better."

A wave of excitement flooded over me. I wasn't isolated any more. I could talk to someone outside this nightmare. I looked at the nurse. Her softness returned and yet, it was apparent something still weighed heavily on her.

I smiled, "Thank you, you've been great. God, this is wonderful. Thank you so much. "

She reached out and I took her hand again. A strange warmth passed between us. It felt almost like an electric buzz. She seemed to sense it too and her features softened again.

"I have to go now, if you're alright? My shift is nearly over and I still have other patients to attend to. You sure you're OK?"

I was much calmer, "I'm better, thanks to you and the phone."

She opened the door but stopped and looked back, "Mr. Clay, would you mind if I came by again? Maybe tonight? I have someone who would like to meet you. If that's alright? Would that be OK?"

"As long as they don't have a needle or a bible, sure. I'd enjoy some rational company."

She left with my sanity trailing closely behind her. Richard's image came back as soon as the door closed and haunted me again. I was somehow the reason he died. I grabbed for the call button once more but as I did, the phone fell on its side and the sound of dial tone filled the room.

I stared at the set for a few moments until a small voice badgered me to hang up. I pushed the receiver button and held it as I wondered what to do next. My friends were gone. I could call clients or suppliers but what would I say? If they'd read the headlines and realized who it was, what the hell *could* I say? "Hey there Bob, got my side shot out. I was the only one left breathing. How's business? By the way, I'm God now. My price is going up."

I searched my mental address book and found only one name; Ellen. I tried, at length, to come up with someone else, anyone else, but Ellen's number haunted me.

It seems that when we need it least, old pain returns to delight in the new.

Hers was the only number I could remember, the only one not just built into my speed dial and who was still alive. We'd shared each other's pain before and though she'd been the reason for most of mine, she was the only person I could think of that I might somehow relate to. I closed my eyes.

A tinny ring came from the receiver, once, twice and as it started to ring a third time I realized my mistake and decided to hang up but a voice answered, "Hello?"

I froze at the sound. "Hello?" she demanded. Someone spoke in the background, she shot back a muffled reply then insisted, "Who is this?"

"Ellen." I said in a broken voice.

"Whoever this is, say something now or get off my phone. It's too damn early to play games."

"Ellen, it's me."

"Jeremy? Is that you?" There was an odd wonder in her voice. "Where are you? What the hell is going on? I saw all this shit on the news. I thought you were probably dead. "

I cringed at her voice. I wanted so badly to hang up and be

done with her, but I answered instead, "It's me." It was too late to go back now, I'd crossed the line.

"Where are you? Everyone wants to know."

Without thinking, I told her about the hospital. "You heard about Richard, then?"

"Yah, saw it on TV. I called KLSR and told them I knew you. Now everyone wants to talk to *me*. Jeremy, I'm a fricken star. They want me for an interview." Her voice became animated and grew louder. The person in the background said something in anger. She muffled the phone but her shrill tone still cut through, "Will you shut the hell up. I'm doing business here, go back to sleep."

She came back, "I'm really glad you called. No one knows where you are. Nobody but me now. Don't tell anybody else. I'll come and see you as soon as I get some cash. Jeremy this is big! But right now I've got to go. It's pretty early and someone's pissed off." She hesitated, "Now, don't you go and get better before I get there." With that she hung up.

I put the phone down, rolled over and bit my lip, adding more pain to my growing misery. I could taste blood by the time I'd relaxed. I trembled at the thought of what I'd wrought upon myself.

I'd reached for a thread of support and it was twisting around my throat. I coughed several times but the tightness remained. "It's time to quit," I thought. It's over. Let it go, lie here and die. Just choke to death on your own stupidity."

A knock at the door brought breakfast.

TWENTY EIGHT

The phone went dead later that morning. After three days I'd finally found a way to reach out, get in touch with the outside world and I'd wasted my opportunity on Ellen. A nurse informed me the entire wing was experiencing a communications problem. Repairs had been implemented during the night. Apparently, several other hospital systems depended on the phone lines and she assured me communications would be back soon.

After I spoke with Ellen, I'd attempted a call to a client but just reached a voice mail that was full. I couldn't even leave a message. Now my brief connection had ended and I still longed to hear a voice I knew.

The day dragged interminably, I wondered if even Kathryn had abandoned me. Several times I pushed the button on my remote for pain medication. Time twisted and distorted but didn't relieve the loneliness.

Around seven P.M. someone knocked at the door. The nurse from my morning anxiety attack looked in. The room seemed to brighten as she stepped through the door.

"I came to see if you were still up for some company?" She

said.

"Dear God, I'd love some. Come in, please, come in." I noticed she wasn't in uniform.

She raised a finger and stepped back out of the door but before I could question, she came back pushing a man in a wheel chair. "Jeremy Clay, I'd like you to meet my father, Avery Carlson."

The man nodded as she wheeled him to my bedside. He was age itself. He might have been a hundred years old, a hundred bad years. He was emaciated and bent. His skin was severely blotched and he had the pallor of a corpse. As she rolled him near, he reached a palsied hand to me and gazed without expression. I looked at his daughter then back to him. He should be her great grandfather.

His hand wavered in the air as he tried to hold it up. I reached out and took it gently, fearful it might shatter. The flesh was dead cold.

I looked at the nurse and started to withdraw my hand when the old man clutched hard. His strength was phenomenal. He almost crushed my fingers and pain crawled up my arm as I tried to pull away. Bones cracked but I couldn't tell if they were mine or his.

I looked at him expecting rage as pressure intensified. His expression seemed to plead as I tried to pull away. The wheel chair rolled closer until his face was inches from mine. His breath was sick and stale. He wheezed, "Help me, please. Everything I have, it's yours. Please."

My heart froze. My hand felt colder than his. I couldn't get air. I was terrified of this old creature pleading, begging me for something.

His grip failed and his hand fell away. I looked to his daughter. She covered her eyes and sobbed. I gazed between the two, the man, then her again and tried to understand what the hell was happening.

Faint voices filtered from beyond the door, somewhere a bell rang. I felt more alone than I ever imagined possible. The room began to darken. My vision faded to a tunnel and all I could see was the man's face. He was a pinpoint of light in a vast darkness. As his image began to fade I thought I saw him smile and form the words, "Thank You."

TWENTY NINE

Someone sat in a chair next to me and read a newspaper by a dim desk lamp. I looked around and found we were alone. She must have heard me rustling because Kathryn lowered the paper and spun toward me, her smile was thrilling.

"You're awake. It's about time. I've been crazy with news for you and all I could do was watch you sleep." She leaned down and kissed me on the cheek. Something I'd nearly forgotten stirred ever so slightly.

"Jeremy, my dear, dear friend, we're on our way." Her enthusiasm poured over me.

"On our way where, to what? Kathryn, please don't do this to me." My voice was that of my childhood, pleading to be released. It irritated me that I could be so weak.

Without reason I was overcome by a memory from years before. It was as though I were there again. Two bullies pulled me off the sidewalk on my way home from school and pummeled me for no apparent reason. One held me while the second punched me, over and over. I couldn't escape, I couldn't fight back. I was at their mercy and they had none. They stopped their onslaught only after I fell limp on the ground and each took one last kick before they left me on a lawn, beaten and helpless.

I was on that lawn again. Powerless, at the mercy of any psycho who chose to beat the hell out of me. I tried to get away to escape. "Jeremy, what's wrong? What the hell are you doing?" Someone grabbed my shoulders and I cringed expecting a fist to fall.

"Jeremy!" Someone shouted directly at my face. "Jeremy! Open your eyes. Look at me. It's Kathryn, look at me!"

I opened my eyes and instead of the sadistic smiles I'd imagined, there was fear. Fear and a sense of concern I'd not thought possible.

I fell back on the bed, exhausted, still near panic. Kathryn's distress grew, "Are you alright? What the hell just happened?"

Control crept back. I closed my eyes shook my head and turned away. "What the hell, do I look OK?" I swallowed. "I can't do this."

"Jeremy, I don't want to imply I know what you're going through. I'm sure it must be devastating, but that's why I'm here. I'm here with you. You're not alone. I'll lead you through all of this. It has to be right. We," she swallowed, "I don't want you to hurt anymore."

I took a deep breath and turned to her, "It's not going to be that easy. Everyone's dead, everything is gone. I have nothing, no income, no home, no friends, absolutely nothing."

"You have me, Jeremy. I'm here for you. And don't worry about money. That's what I've been burning to tell you. Everything is covered. If you were standing up, I'd ask you to sit down because this'll knock you on your ass."

She reached into her jacket pocket, pulled out her hand then patted the left one. She put her head down and smiled, "I quit smoking."

She walked to the foot of my bed and started talking wildly, waving her hands in the air as she spoke. "This is going to be hard to believe but you have to. I'm not insane. Just listen. Don't worry about your business. The old saying, doors close and others open. You've got an entirely new job ahead of you as soon as you're ready. "

She became even more animated and rambled about my 'new job'.

"Kathryn, slow down. I told you, I'm not a Messiah and I won't lie to everyone. It just won't work, it's not right. No one's going to buy it, especially not from me. No one will ever believe it."

She stopped and looked at me, eyes wide, "Jeremy, you don't understand."

I found myself shouting, "No. You don't understand. This is asinine. People will see right through it. They'll know it's a lie the first time I open my mouth and sure as hell, some asshole is going to get pissed and shoot me again. Listen to me! I don't want any part of it. Find someone else!"

She came back to my side and took my hand. "Calm down, listen to me, please. I can't begin to imagine how frightening this must be. Trust me that it's not just some reality show. This is big. Bigger than you could ever imagine. It's not just you and me. There are entire nations behind this. It has a life of its own."

I pulled away from her, "I won't do it. It's all bullshit As soon as I can get the hell out of here I'm gone. I'll disappear and start over. That's all I want. I just want to be me again."

She spoke in a tone so quiet I could barely hear her, "I know, you're scared. Just let me ..."

"Let you what? You've already done too damn much. Hear what I'm saying; NO. If you really want to help me, tell them I'm dead...or tell them I'm the damn Devil if you have to. I'm not their Christ. They need to find someone else and that's that."

"Dammit Jeremy, please listen to me. It's a living, growing

entity and there is no way you can quit, it's impossible. Trust me, it doesn't matter where you go, what you do, you can't quit. I didn't do this, I'm just the messenger. It's gotten too fucking big and gone too fucking far. You have no choice, you have to deal with it."

She took a breath and pushed her hair back. "Listen, I can't argue with you right now. I'm your friend and I'm trying…"

I shouted louder, "Friend? Friend? They tried to kill me and you've made me a freak. My entire life's been destroyed, I'm on the edge of crazy and you want to throw me in the middle of a fucking fairytale. How long do you think I'll live when I get out there? There's probably a thousand raving, pissed off assholes right this moment, who want to blow my brains out the first chance they get. What kind of friend would do that?"

She looked at me in shock, her fight gone. The excitement she'd brought faded along with the sparkle in her eyes. It looked as though I'd physically beaten her and I suddenly realized that I wasn't fighting some pricks from my childhood, I was attacking the only true friend I had left.

My anger was sucked into a whirlpool of despair, "I'm sorry. I didn't mean … I don't want this, but … I didn't want…I don't want to lose you. I'm so sorry. I need you. You're the only one I have left, the only person still here."

I was bound by her beauty. I couldn't bear to lose anyone else, especially her. The last thing I wanted was to force her away.

"The problem is, the only time you're here is when you want to sell me this Messiah shit. I can't deal with that, I need more than that…from you." I rolled away and faced the wall.

The bed sagged as she sat and slid her arm over me. "Jeremy, I didn't want to leave you here by yourself, but I've been working my ass off to control the mania and protect you. If I hadn't, everything would have gone straight to hell and become as ugly as you could possibly imagine. I had to be there to save it, to save you. There *were* people who wanted to crucify you. Oh God, I didn't…you know what I mean. They wanted to hurt you." I looked back at her and saw tears in her eyes.

"Honestly, I did not create this. There's no way on earth I could have created this. I wouldn't have done that to you even if I could. It has a life of its own and if I hadn't pulled every string available, if I hadn't orchestrated things in the very best way possible, it would have been a disaster. Believe me, we've done everything we can to make this as stable as possible."

"The media was digging through your entire life within hours of the shooting. They wanted to prove it all wrong. Fanatics came out in droves to destroy what some were calling the new Jesus. We had to establish a support system, someone who could deal with the threats and put a stop to them."

She leaned against my shoulder. "You've got to realize one thing. Richard and Maggie put everything on the line for the truth. No one planned to die, but it happened. They died wanting to change the world. They did what was right."

She looked into my eyes and continued. "At the same time, thousands saw you as the focus of the movement, the answer to their prayers. Despite everyone who wanted to stop you, the belief took hold and pockets of people everywhere began to believe in and accept you. Right now, you're the hope of millions everywhere. This country, the world, they need you to be who they believe you to be."

She fell silent and leaned on my shoulder sobbing. She had apparently worked nonstop since I last saw her. She seemed frustrated and exhausted. She cried until she became limp against me. I rolled back toward her and took her in my arms. My strength returned as I held her. She looked up, hesitated, then kissed me passionately. The hospital, the lies, the madness faded as we came together. All that existed was the warmth. I lay back with her on top of me.

Although her weight and the movement were painful, neither of us hesitated.

THIRTY

I choked down the last piece of dry chicken, followed it with warm water then swung the tray to the side. I shifted my weight several times to find a comfortable position but to no avail. Finally, unable to resolve the aches, I dragged my feet over the edge of the bed and forced myself to sit up. I was weak and had difficulty breathing but it was wonderful to finally see the world vertically again.

I lifted myself, with support of the handrail, and stood somewhat erect. I felt like a man of ninety. When I found my balance I reached for the stand that held my I.V. and shuffled a few inches toward the bathroom. Someone knocked at the door. A nurse peeked in.

"Mr. Clay? I'm sorry to bother you but there's a woman here," She looked at a scrap of paper in her hand. "Her name is...uhm...Ellen Frasier. She insists that you asked her here and she's making quite a scene. We have instructions to prohibit unauthorized visitors but she insists that you told her to come." She raised her eyebrows to emphasize 'insists'.

"The duty supervisor thought we might want to check with

you before we call the authorities."

I shook my head, cringed, fell back to the bed and immediately looked around for an escape route. There was none.

"Mr. Clay?"

"Oh hell." I sighed. "You might as well let her in. The worse she can do is kill me."

She nodded hesitantly and looked confused.

"Just joking, send her up. Better me than the rest of the hospital."

I pulled my feet back on the bed, laid down, and waited. I felt like a condemned man after my last meal. I wished I'd told Kathryn about my mistake. Ever since the call, I'd prayed Ellen wouldn't find the money to leave Michigan. But apparently, she had. I'd actually invited this torment back into my life so I slapped myself, hard on the forehead. A voice inside said, "Another fine mess you've gotten me into, Ollie," and I wanted to hit myself again, but closed my eyes and waited for the warden to lead me to my death.

A knock on the door startled me back and Ellen sauntered through the doorway and up to my side.

She wore a bright red, Asian dress that appeared to be from a 1930's Dashiell Hammett movie. Her long dark hair swayed invitingly as she leaned over me. My heart pounded in my ears as I watched helplessly. She had me trapped and she knew it.

Feelings erupted, started as a kernel of loathing and grew like ivy, entangling me with disgust. Anger sparked and my pain smoldered with so much heat I felt my side might burst into flame.

"Jeremy. My God you look like shit." She smiled. "You told me you were all right. You sure don't look 'all right'."

I breathed deep, closed my eyes and shook my head.

"Oh Jeremy, don't start. I was really worried when I heard what happened. It's just that they said you …that…well, I just expected you to look a lot better. Was it horrible?" She reached into her bag and pulled a disc. "I made a copy for you. They cut a lot on TV, but I got the entire video off the net. You can see what happened to Richard and all the others. They have lots of angles and slow motion. I felt so bad…"

"Ellen Please", I tried to shout but my strength suddenly wilted and all that came out was breath..

She looked irritated, as though I'd slapped her. She put the disc down on the table. "Listen Jeremy, I didn't come here so you could be pissy with me. I thought you'd like to see the whole thing from another viewpoint."

I inhaled, paused a moment and spoke softly, "Ellen, I have neither the energy nor the desire to continue this. I'm sorry you came all this way for nothing. I'm truly sorry I asked you here. It's not going to work. I don't know what I was thinking. I apologize. Just go home. It was wrong, really wrong."

She glared at me in silence, her complexion reddened and a wisp of a smile touched her lips. I could see she wanted the games again but I didn't care. I turned away.

"It's not over just yet…Mr. Messiah."

I squeezed my eyes tight and felt like I was being strapped in the electric chair.

"You left me in quite a bind last spring. No job, no car, no cash. I had to do some pretty desperate things to make ends meet. I had to kiss a lot of ass to get back on track. I'm still not there, Jeremy. I still have some catch up to do, but things are looking brighter now. You've got some scam going here don't you? Whatever it is, I'm in. You owe me."

I glared back at her in disbelief, "Look at me. Does it look like I have any money? My business is gone, I'm a ward of the government, maybe you can ask *them* for cash."

"You left me, Jeremy-boy. You dumped me in the street."

"Don't give me that. I took care of you for years. I asked you over and over to get a job but you were more than comfortable living off me. I owe you nothing. I'm not your meal ticket anymore. Get the hell out of here and leave me alone."

Her smile heightened and I could almost taste her bitterness. "Let me tell you a little story first. Last Monday after I called the TV station, some men came to my house. They asked a shitload of questions about you, Jeremy. They offered me a thousand dollars just for information. They were there for more than an hour badgering me, trying to get me to sign some papers. They thought they were slick, but the joke's on them, I'm smarter than they think I am. I refused to talk to them for a lousy grand and I told them to get the hell out until they could come up with a decent offer."

She became serious, "I know how big this is. You've been on the news every day. All the shit usually disappears real quick, but they're still talking about you on every station. I could smell the money."

She paced the room but kept her eyes fixed on me. "You and I both know that this is about money. You might get a book deal, maybe even a movie. If you do, I could star in it. You do some of those miracles they keep talking about and I'll smile pretty and look surprised."

She glowered, "Whatever it is Jeremy, something big's about to happen. I don't know your angle yet, but I know it's filled with cash, lots and lots of cash, and I won't be left out."

She hesitated while she built her case, "I couldn't believe you had the stones to come up with something this weird, but I intend to be your shadow from now on. I'll be attached to you when the checks come in. And when they do, believe me, I'll get my share. You can take that to the bank." She laughed.

She loomed over me and looked down, "No, dear Jeremy. We are definitely not done yet. You and I have a lot of golden time left together. If you try to screw me out of my half, I'll sell you out so quick your head'll spin. Wait! Can't do that one," she chuckled, "they already did it in 'The Exorcist'. We'll have to come up with something new."

Her voice hardened, "I'm either in your little plan or I take you down. I'm sure I can get a hell of a lot more than a lousy thousand dollars if I tell them what a pin dick, asshole you are. You better think about that one, sweetie."

I looked up in awe, "Blackmail?"

She leaned over and whispered, "Let's not be so ugly, let's call it...palimony. You owe me. You pull in the bucks and I'll manage the finances. Kinda' like the old days... We'll both be better off. And hey, don't forget the fringe benefits." She wiggled her shoulders, "It's gonna' work out just fine."

The door opened and Kathryn stepped through, "Am I interrupting?" She asked quietly, ready for a confrontation.

I was able to breathe again. It felt like a last minute reprieve. "No, not at all. Please! Come in."

I introduced them, "Kathryn, this is Ellen Frasier from Ann Arbor. Ellen is just leaving, aren't you Ellen?" I glared toward her.

"I suppose." She smiled at Kathryn and turned back to me, "I'll be back when you you're not so busy. And just know, Jeremy, I'm here for you. I'm staying with a friend of a friend here in Virginia. Don't worry, I'll be in touch."

As she walked past Kathryn she glowered, "Watch out for this one. He can be a real pain in the ass. He'll dump you without a word." She stopped, "Besides, I'm not quite done with him yet." She opened the door and turned back, "See you soon sweetheart." then walked out.

"What the hell was that about? How in God's name did she get in here?"

I proceeded to explain what I had done and what Ellen had said.

"What is she blackmailing you for? What can she offer them?

Jeremy, have you done something hideous we're not aware of?"

"You want to know my most hideous offence? Bringing her back into my life, that's the stupidest thing I've ever done. She has nothing, but that won't stop her. She's evil, she'll say anything and invent shit if she thinks she can make a dime from it."

Kathryn stepped toward the hallway and pulled out her cell phone as she exited. I was curious since the area was supposed to be a dead zone.

I could hear her talking through the door. She sounded concerned and after a moment, spoke a bit too loud. I heard her say, "Hunter was right. Let him know. We need to take care of this ASAP." A moment later she returned and dropped the phone in her purse.

I looked at her, "What was that? Who's going to take care of what?"

She looked over her shoulder toward the door, "We have people in DC who need this to work. They're invested in the belief you can pacify some of the world's tensions. They don't want issues that cause problems and might upset everything they've done. You're the key to this. You have an international following now. If something horrible came out it could be a major setback Believe me, everyone wants you safe. They won't allow some minor crook to distract things with blackmail."

She patted her pockets searching for her cigarettes "Ellen's been a concern for some time. Hunter made her an offer to keep her quiet but she got dollar signs in her eyes and refused to sign a non-disclosure. They've been monitoring her but she disappeared yesterday. It was a complete surprise when she showed up here. Hospital staff contacted us as soon as she threatened them. We decided to let her see you to find what she has in mind. They wanted to know if she still cared for you or if she wanted to lean on you."

She shook her head, "It seems she hasn't missed you as much as she let on. She just made a huge mistake and implicated herself in felony blackmail."

She sat on the bed and pushed my hair back with her hand, "Don't worry, there'll be no problem. That woman has a patchy record and now she's added a federal offence. This time their offer will consist of how many years she wants to spend in prison. She'll be allowed to go back to Michigan and if she's smart and behaves, she'll continue to be free. If not... Either way, you won't have to worry about her again. If she has any sense, she'll see her wicked ways and maybe even grow from all of this."

THIRTY ONE

Early Thursday morning, nine days after the shooting, I was to be released from the hospital.

I was nervous, extremely nervous. Television, radio and the press had elevated everything to a crescendo over the past week and a half. Speculation about the mysterious Jeremy Clay was everywhere. Stories came from around the world of appearances and miracles. People demanded to see me.

A press conference was scheduled for the afternoon. I no longer had a choice. I wondered when the truth would be discovered and what would happen to me after, but Kathryn assured me I would be protected and my future safety would be assured.

I scanned some of the week's articles about this Jeremy Clay. I read quotes about peace and forgiveness. The picture of this man, no, much more than a man, still graced the papers. The bloodied hands raised in the air to sooth a raging crowd, the soft indefinable glow that seemed to emanate from within, the eyes that radiated complete tranquility and an enthralling essence of love.

The photos were perfect, like none I'd ever seen. If I didn't know better I would have assumed they were Photoshopped, however, they came from several cameras and multiple angles and all reflected the same sense. I wished for it to be true, but longed for someone else to be the one who would bring comfort to the world. Instead, they were my eyes looking back.

The newspaper trembled in my hands as reality seized me again. *My* eyes, my *mortal* eyes gazed from the page while everyone expected a Savior. My hands shook so hard the paper fell and pages fluttered down to fan out on the floor.

I whispered, "They've got it all wrong. When they see me, when they hear me, they'll all know. They're looking at a damned picture and listening to stories. They'll know the truth. Everyone will know."

I leaned against the wall and shuddered uncontrollably. A stack of papers covered the table next to me. They came from major cities around the globe. My photo stared at me from each one and each spoke of 'The Messiah' in different languages. They all wanted answers to questions but not one denied the claim.

My stomach turned so I took several deep breaths to force the panic out.

A gentle knock on the door drew me away. A nurse entered

with yet another newspaper.

"Mr. Clay? I'm sorry if I'm disturbing you but I thought you might like to see this before your breakfast comes." I nodded and she placed her gift on the pile.

"I have something else for you." She reached into her pocket, took out an envelope and held it out to me.

"Linda Carlson, the night nurse, asked me to give this to you. It's from her father. She was suspended for bringing him here so she begged me to be sure you got this before you left. Normally, I wouldn't, but considering what happened....I mean, how could I say no?" She smiled wide, "None of us could believe it." She hesitated and reddened a bit. "I'm, I'm really sorry. I mean, we believe it but it was just so....well, you know."

I shook my head and replied, "No, I don't know. What happened?"

"Linda's father? Didn't they tell you?' She looked surprised, "After you touched him. He went into total remission. He's completely healed, like the others. The doctors don't know what to say. We were all in shock."

Tremors flowed through me again, the envelope slipped to the bed. She placed her fingers on my shoulder, squeezed gently and turned to leave. At the door she looked back, "I thank God that I've been blessed by being with you these past several days." She quickly disappeared through the door and it closed behind her.

My breath had stopped again and I gasped. The envelope lay on the bed beside me. I picked it up and held it at eye level.

That man was nearly dead. It wasn't me. They must have done something or he did. All I tried to do was get away from him. I looked at the picture on the front page of the paper the nurse just delivered. Haunting eyes still stared back serenely through a soft glow. Chills climbed my back up to my neck. My entire head began to tingle and loud ringing filled in my ears. I looked at the thick envelope, frightened to open it, horrified at what I might find.

After half an hour of nervous contemplation I placed the unopened envelope in the drawer of the side table. I couldn't find the courage to see what it said. I pulled a paper from the stack and turned the page to hide my image. The day's news unfolded and I tried to dissolve into someone else's story. I found solace in the rest of the world and read everything that didn't apply to me.

When I turned a page I found a hole cut in the shape of a square. It was among news stories and not likely an advertisement or coupon. I looked at the back to see what was missing from the other side. An article about a storm in the Caribbean was cut in two.

I disregarded it and continued to read. After a few seconds, I was assaulted by a frightening thought. I threw the paper to the floor and picked up another. After leafing through several pages I found another hole. I dropped it and continued searching. Of nine American newspapers, six had items cut from them, all near the continuation of stories about me. It was suddenly apparent something was being kept from me. I reeled and tried to imagine what might be so horrible they wouldn't want me to see it.

It came like a slap in the face. "Assassination." Of course, there were those who wanted me dead. I began to panic and searched for a way to escape. Though still in a hospital gown, I rushed for the door. With a hand on the doorknob, I stopped. "They might be out there, waiting." I put my hand to my forehead and tried to think.

"Calm down, calm down" I repeated over and over. I returned to the bed and rested until the fear began to subside. Kathryn assured me I was safe here. I decided my best option was to stay here, surrounded by people who supported me. I tried to reason away the missing articles and after a time my breathing began to respond, the terror decreased and cautious assurance returned.

"How the hell am I going to do this? I'm already going crazy and I haven't even made an appearance yet." I lay back and felt as though I were on death row again, this time with no possibility of reprieve.

A knock on the door caused me to gasp. I inadvertently choked and coughed deeply. When the door opened there was a breakfast cart, wheeled by a nurse and Kathryn. They glanced at one another as conspirators and Kathryn whispered in the nurse's ear and closed the door behind them.

"Good morning Mr. Clay. How are you today?" An unusually bright smile bloomed across the nurse's face.

"Jeremy, I hope you had a good night, we have quite a day ahead of us." Kathryn came closer, "Personally, I didn't sleep at all. I haven't been able to for three days. I'm running on pure adrenalin." She bent forward and kissed my cheek.

"Kathryn, I found something in the papers…"

"Mr. Clay," the nurse interrupted, "Since this is the last time we we'll be able to serve you breakfast, the staff decided to make it something special. It isn't quite hospital policy so I hope you'll enjoy what we've prepared."

She pulled the bed tray around, removed a cover and placed

a plate in front of me. She took a vase with flowers from under the cart followed by a bottle of Dom Perignon, and two champagne flutes. Her smile grew with her excitement and at the same time, my concerns faded. Kathryn peeled the cover and the wire from the bottle and popped the cork. It erupted, striking the ceiling. They both cheered quietly.

The nurse said, "It's been a great honor to serve you these past several days. I'll never forget this time, thank you."

Her eyes reflected the emotion with which she spoke. There was no hospital frivolity, no artificial bedside manner. She appeared absolutely genuine and sincere.

I reached for her hand and she trembled. "Thank *you* for everything. Thanks for this fantastic meal. I won't forget you either."

I meant what I said. I would never forget the look of serenity and joy on her face. She shook my hand, nodded and left the room. My fears about the paper faded with the occasion as I delighted in Kathryn's smile.

"Thanks again, Betty. Please remind everyone we'll need the next few hours without interruption." The door closed as the nurse left and Kathryn filled the flutes and raised her glass for a toast. I lifted the other and held it out.

She said, "To a long and wonderful relationship, and all the peace we can create."

We tapped glasses and drank. "If you don't mind?" I pointed to the breakfast.

"By all means, don't you dare let it get cold." She refilled my glass, "You have no idea what I went through to get it here."

I began to devour the meal, "Can I offer you something? I feel guilty eating all this in front of you."

"No, it's all yours, enjoy it, that's why I brought it here." She sipped from her glass as I ate.

When my glass was empty, she filled it again before she spoke, "Jeremy, I have the changes you asked for. We need to go over everything again before the press conference. Remember, just follow the suggestions and try not to make any concrete statements today, nothing you'll be held accountable for later."

She unlocked her briefcase, removed a notebook and opened it. "We need to stay with generalities. The pollsters will follow up and determine our strongest path. If you get a question that's too direct, we'll change the course and….."

"Kathryn, you can't imagine how terrified I've been about this. It all sounds so...so wrong, so dishonest."

"Jeremy, listen it's not dishonest. You'll never say anything you don't agree with. It's just that your first encounter with media wolves can be traumatic. They all want headlines. If we allow them to bait you or take words out of context, they'll twist everything you say just to get their bylines. You have a huge following but there are still some who want you to fail. If they can find a means to discredit you and take your power, they'll do it. We want to avoid that.'

She sipped her wine, "We've planned every contingency we could imagine to make this as safe as possible. If you're to survive long enough to develop credibility, we need to control conditions; the questions and the answers. We'll do everything we can to protect you from being seen as a fool or a charlatan."

"But Kathryn, I am a charlatan! And if I go through with this I'm a fool, too"

She poured more champagne into my glass and motioned for me to drink. "Jeremy, understand this. It's gone beyond whether or not you want this. It's here and there's no safe way to turn back. What you say today will affect thousands, excuse me, millions. You're not a movie star or some game show host who'll hand out money or embarrass someone. You won't be forgotten in a week. It's much, much more than 15 minutes of fame. Realize this; there are enough followers at this very moment to start international riots with the wrong direction. You're a phenomenon. We need to go slow and steady until we know how well you'll be accepted."

I drained the glass and she filled it again. "People who truly believe in icons like you've become, are willing to die for those beliefs. Worse yet, they're willing to kill for them. Like it or not, you're that significant. Not only what you say, but how you say it, could have extreme consequences."

I sat there, glass in hand, champagne sloshed over the rim of the flute as it moved with my exaggerated breathing.

"Don't waste that, drink up." She said, "I need you relaxed so we can cover everything again."

I looked into the glass of bursting bubbles, tipped it up and drank. I couldn't tell if the champagne was affecting me or relieving my anxiety, but I could no longer think about being The Messiah. My focus turned to Kathryn. All I could see were her eyes. She continued to speak but I didn't listen. I wanted to escape into her again, for maybe the last time.

I watched as she read from her notebook. I reached out, took it and dropped it to the floor. "Jeremy, there isn't…" I pushed the tray table away, took her hand and pulled her to the bed. She seemed surprised but didn't resist. I wrapped my arms around her and pulled her into an embrace.

She joined me in a kiss then said, "Pretty insistent for a wounded man." I heard shoes drop as she kicked them to the floor. She was with me, and nothing existed but her. Our breathing connected as we became one. The world was as it should be. I knew her. I loved her. I trusted her.

THIRTY TWO

That evening I sat on a stage before nearly thirty members of the media in a room cluttered with assistants, microphones and cameras. Kathryn, at the front of the audience, acted as my focal point. Security personnel guarded the wings, roamed the floor and two more flanked me on the stage. A teleprompter was hidden near the floor in front of me. I looked at Kathryn and our rehearsal played over and over in my mind. Although the champagne's effect was gone, warmth still surrounded me and helped relieve some of the tension. The questions were prescreened and I felt fairly confident with the answers.

The responses, provided by a team of political writers, were designed to provide information that implied an answer while remaining non-committal.

I chose to sit for my own comfort. A woman stepped forward and quieted the crowd, introduced herself as the moderator, then presented me. When the reporters offered subdued applause, nervousness started to rise and I looked to Kathryn, sure the panic showed on my face. She smiled gently and nodded.

The moderator explained the session would be strictly a

question and answer period and it had to be kept brief.

The floor was opened to questions and the moderator pointed to a man near the front.

He was immediately direct and to the point, "What makes you believe you're the Son of God?"

Although we expected the question and prepared for it, It hit me like a slap in the face. I took a deep breath and internally reviewed my prepared answers but everything was jumbled. I looked to Kathryn and she tipped her eyes to the teleprompter. I glanced down and began to recite "Several days ago I was witness to a great tragedy. Lives were lost. Many more might have been. I stepped forward to protect the crowd. Several of those present felt great peace in the midst of chaos. Those people offered their personal experiences. "

He countered, "So you deny the idea that you're a Messiah?"

I swallowed, sure my gulp was caught on camera, "I have never offered claims to that effect. I defer to those who were present at the time. It was them who made the assertions."

Another reporter was called. "It's been said that you've visited hundreds of people around the world over the past several days. We've seen vague photos but no confirmation that you were at any of these places. Is it a fact that you've appeared around the globe? How is that possible considering the fact that you can't even stand here today?"

I stood from the stool and looked into his eyes. The questions were already beginning to stray from those presented "I won't impugn those who had an experience. Only they know their truth, I refuse to deny their beliefs."

"So you're saying these reports were spurious. You admit you didn't perform the miracles attributed to you?"

I glanced to the teleprompter for help. The moderator came forward to address the rising cacophony, "Excuse me, but ..."

Someone shouted, "They say you healed dying people. How do you respond to that?"

"I don't claim...," before I could answer, questions began to burst like shots from an assault rifle, staccato and each one louder.

"Are you saying the reports are lies?"

The moderator raised her voice. I smiled at her, took her shoulder and gently moved her aside. Kathryn was overcome with panic. She jumped from her chair and rushed to the stage stairs.

I raised my left hand to her, then to the crowd. Through the noise and confusion all eyes focused on me. The room quieted instantly.

My fear calmed as I recalled the rich warmth that visited me in Washington. I spoke softly, nearly whispered, "I repeat, I never made those claims, however, I don't refute their validity."

The reporters were fixed on me. Cameras flashed, video rolled and the room was silent.

Kathryn, eyes wide, stared from the edge of the stage as someone shouted, "Mr. Clay, What is your role, your purpose in all of this? Why do you think this is unfolding as it is?"

The answer rolled from me, "Our world has recently been immersed in untold tragedy. These horrible events can either unite people or bring destruction to all we know."

"I didn't choose to be part of the devastation nor did I choose to be the forerunner of change. I only know I'm now in a position to help unite humanity and help bring an end to the suffering."

"The world must decide what they believe, who I am and what I've accomplished. I make no claims but I accept the role thrust upon me and will do whatever I can to help bring peace to all."

Ten minutes later, the time was up, and I realized I hadn't used the teleprompter at all after the first question. I forgot what Kathryn and I discussed beforehand, but answers seemed to flow naturally. Although, I was confident her prompting was ingrained somewhere in my subconscious, I'd done it all on my own.

As reporters were escorted out and I exited the stage, the concern I had about my position had begun to evaporate until we left the hall. Thousands lined the street, waiting for me. Security ushered us to a waiting car holding back throngs of followers. Everyone along the path strained to touch me. I finally understood the significance of the situation.

We were chauffeured through the masses while thousands of hands squeaked against the windows and doors as we passed. My newly found confidence was quickly overcome by a shroud of claustrophobia. We finally reached the road to the airport and I was afflicted with violent shaking.

At 70 miles per hour, together in the darkness of the back of the car, Kathryn took my hand and gently kissed me. "You did it Jeremy Clay. You did it."

THIRTY THREE

The next afternoon we relaxed in a motel room, hidden in the heart of a vast corn field traversed by a ribbon of highway. Huge semi-trucks traveled incessantly both East and West.

Kathryn and I dined on blocks of processed steak, powdered potatoes and small square cobs of corn from the motel restaurant. In this vast farm belt, the cradle of America, we ate cardboard replicas of the real food that grew just outside our door.

We sipped generic wine and waited for the evening news on a combination TV/clock radio, bolted to the dresser. Apparently the motel was concerned someone might steal it for its ghost images and static. Kathryn told me about our team members on the flight here. They planned to join us, help evaluate our presentation and determine its impact. They were bringing poll information to appraise the responses and improve the message. Our isolation was a buffer in case something had gone wrong. They wanted time to regroup if necessary, before any further appearances.

On the morning news, eyewitnesses claimed they experienced my presence in three locations around the globe since I spoke yesterday evening.

Several people from a small village in Romania believed I'd saved 28 miners trapped by a cave-in just six hours after the conference. A village of more than one thousand in Sri Lanka claimed I appeared to them in the sky after an earthquake and led them to safety through the darkness like a morning star. The station cut to a scene from the stage in Virginia. The camera panned to a close up of me.

My words and image were somehow captivating, almost as though I'd been digitized to create some ethereal image. It was me, they were my words, but the entire scene was somehow mesmerizing, beguiling. I studied my image as it spoke and was enthralled. I couldn't turn away. After a few moments another voice broke through; the most reverend Thomas Singleton appeared on screen. I shook my head as they explained that Singleton held his own press conference to reflect on this Jeremy Clay.

"Here we go," Kathryn clasped my arm, "your sternest critic." She smiled at me and turned back to the TV.

"….have come to believe that there is a compelling wisdom in Mr. Clay's statements. Though I don't espouse him to be the revivification, he seems to hold to the truths I and my followers have been affirming all along. At first I was doubtful, however Mr. Clay has not forsaken the Word nor has he cast doubt on the beliefs we all cherish. I, therefore, lend my support and encouragement to…"

"Singleton?" I was shocked. "I don't believe it. He's a freak. I don't want that asshole supporting me! What the hell? What's he after?"

Kathryn shushed me and nodded toward the television. She increased the volume with the remote.

"…call my followers to join me and Mr. Clay in unity to bring about our goals of peace and advance Christianity through the world.

"I have yet to personally meet with Mr. Clay," He kept calling me 'Mr. Clay'. I was livid that he would associate me with his rabid hatefulness, but I continued to listen. "…however, I'm encouraged that he supports me and my followers in developing the type of world that we know to be apposite. Mr. Clay…" Each time he said my name I clenched my teeth. "is on our squad. As team mates, we must all encourage and support him.

"Mr. Clay will join me here at the Palace of Light to share our hopes and desires. So we can unite and be affirmed through the Word of our Lord and promote the Works of Christ."

As Kathryn sensed my anger, her smile grew into an uncontrollable laugh. She lay back on the bed and shook with delight at my complete and utter irritation. "What the hell is so...." she placed her fingers to my lips and with her other hand, pointed at the TV.

The co-anchor continued, "...shocked the nation as several other officials, from diverse denominations, followed suit and offered their support for Jeremy Clay.

"The archdiocese of New York announced this morning that although the Catholic Church hasn't acknowledged Clay to be the Messiah, they support his basic philosophy. Their spokesman stated the church will explore all considerations before they make any formal decisions. Rome has yet to comment, however, they have not renounced..."

Kathryn reached for the remote, muted the noise and hugged me. "We're in." she laughed, "We're legit. Two days ago Singleton bashed you, today he stands fully beside you. Your biggest opponent is now courting your approval as the churches begin to take us seriously."

I looked at her as though she were mad, "You mean religions are buying into this?"

"At least, they're not opposing you in public. It's as immense as I said. We are now in control. "

She kissed me then rested her head on my chest, "We have to get started. The team will be here shortly. You'll finally get to meet your staff." She, pointed the remote toward the TV and with a click, the screen went black. She stepped into the bathroom.

"Who is this staff? I mean, where did you find them? This is all too crazy, beyond reality. I need to know what the hell's going on, who's doing what and why. I might have some sort of staff handling things, but if the shit hits the fan, it's me who'll get buried in it. For my sake, I need more information."

The door closed and Kathryn spoke from inside, "Please relax. Over the next few days you'll meet everyone and we'll cover everything. From here on out you'll be part of every decision. It's your ballgame and we work for you. Everyone's here to make sure things move in the right direction and that you have all the support you need."

There were a few moments of silence, the toilet flushed and Kathryn returned. "We've gone through endless preparation to take you public in an acceptable way. You haven't been in the best condition lately so I had to make decisions. I recruited some great people, friends and colleagues, who wanted to help. It had to be orchestrated properly or it would have been a monster." She kissed me again, "I think you'll be impressed with what we've accomplished, just look at the news. The process will be turned over to you now. Our only purpose is to assist."

I thought a moment and asked, "I don't mean to be rude, but what's in it for you? You and your team?"

She looked down and closed her eyes. "I've been waiting for this. Let me explain. Appalling things have happened these past few months. Horrible things we never could have imagined. A city leveled, thousands dead, a president who may have allowed the sacrifice of Americans. Near nuclear annihilation. We witness more and more innocent deaths each and every day, with mass murders and suicide bombers, and why?"

"It has to stop or the earth will end up a ball of shit. If we do nothing we concede to the maniacs who'll continue to destroy us all. You appeared from nowhere, dropped into circumstances beyond your control. With you came hope. With hope came support and the possibility to take this world back from the mad men. How in God's name could I not be part of this? How could anyone turn away from this opportunity?"

Her eyes were wild with excitement. I trusted her implicitly. When she paused a moment, I leaned across to kiss her. We both jumped when someone banged on the door. Kathryn looked through the security hole, undid the latches and allowed a couple in and they all hugged one another.

One raised his eyebrows and smiled my way as he removed his coat and handed it to Kathryn. She placed it on the back of a chair and introduced us, "Annette, Phil, meet Jeremy Clay." Kathryn gleamed as though she were presenting a new lover to her family. I stood to greet them and their outstretched hands.

"Jeremy, meet Annett Thackery and Phillip Allen. They are key figures on your team." Kathryn stepped back as I approached.

Annette had a vivid presence. She appeared older than the rest of us, grey highlighted her short dark hair. She lent an air of sanity to the circumstances. I was comforted to know she was on my side. She took my hand and squeezed, "Happy to finally meet you in person. Although I feel I've known you for a lifetime."

"I've truly been looking forward to this." Phil said as he shook my hand. He seemed to be in his mid-thirties and despite his élan, he retained a friendly, boyish look that made me want to tussle his sandy hair.

"These two were both executives from my first position. Annette was my mentor and Phillip my instructor. When I called them they gave up everything to join me."

She looked at them and said, "We just heard Singleton on the news. Tell me everything."

Phil started, "It was very strange." He looked around, "There wouldn't be any coffee would there?"

"Sure. Let me get you a cup. Annette?"

The attorney shook her head 'no' and Kathryn went toward the bathroom. Phil continued, "We met with the Most Reverend Mr. Singleton this morning in Dallas."

"I'll have you know that Dallas is quite a bit warmer than that man. He's one cold devil." Annette laughed and shook her head, "Tell them about the office."

"My God, Kathryn, it's a fortress." Kathryn returned with a Styrofoam cup and handed it to Phillip, "Thanks," he took a sip, "We were put through metal detectors, sniffed by dogs and even frisked by his minions. That was before we were allowed through the gates. And I do mean gates."

He took another sip, "His compound is surrounded by dual fences. The outer one is covered in concertina wire and the inside fence has an electric charge. He has motion detectors and cameras everywhere, even in the bathrooms. This man is paranoid."

Annette sat in the room's only arm chair, "After we were processed in, a twenty minute ordeal in itself, we were introduced to the man. He seemed rather ill at ease with us. Mr. Hunter apparently had quite an impression on him."

I looked at Kathryn at the mention of Hunter. She offered a brief glance but focused on Annette, who continued, "It took all I had not to laugh in the face of that self-righteous son of a bitch."

"Annette?" Kathryn looked at her in dismay.

"Wait. You'd have to meet him, to physically sit in his presence. The man acts as though he *wrote* the Bible. As if there should be Singleton 1-1, 'Whatever I sayeth is gospel and all others shall bow before me'."

Phil joined in, "She isn't exaggerating. The man is so full of himself it's frightening. He's a monster and, sadly enough, his people fully validate everything he says. I couldn't believe their subservience. But then, I suppose a few hundred million dollars buys a lot of allegiance."

Annette continued, "After we began, it was like talking to an obstinate rock. He made it apparent we were only there because he was forced to see us. He read through his papers while we talked. All the while, his minions came and went. They whispered in his ear, as though we didn't exist. When Phil mentioned Hunter, he finally looked up. He was oh, so angry.

"We passed the proposal and discussed terms. By the time we finished we had his complete attention. Money seems to have quite an impact on him. I suppose you can never have too much. We were escorted from his presence for twenty minutes while he, I'm sure, did everything he possibly could to have us executed. When we were finally ushered back in, his attitude had altered considerably."

I suddenly found myself face to face with Phil, "What's this about money? You offered to finance this asshole? What the hell's going on here?"

Kathryn took my shoulder and eased me back a step. "Jeremy, let me explain."

She leaned close, "I suppose I should have discussed this earlier. It's not what you think. Annette, please start from the top and explain the Singleton proposal."

Annette took my arm and led me to the table. We sat facing one another on miserable straight backed chairs. Phil removed papers from his briefcase and spread them in front of me.

"First of all, Singleton is the obnoxious head of a multimillion dollar business. For some unknown reason, people donate hard earned cash to him. In turn, his organization supports a college, homes for battered wives and an adoption system for unwed mothers. Those 'services' help hundreds if not thousands of people. There are other programs as well.

"But by no means, do all the donations go toward his charitable functions. The IRS became extremely interested in Singleton Industries..., excuse me, Ministries. It seems a high ranking government official had pressed tax agents to be somewhat liberal in their interpretation of Singleton's personal returns.

"Senate investigations dredged up a few very uncomfortable questions. Phil shuffled the papers and pointed to a paragraph. "As you can see, we didn't offer him any assurance of continued income, however the IRS has agreed not to dig further into past returns if he supports you. Mr. Singleton and his advisors saw the huge advantage he might gain."

"Ultimately, Singleton confessed his condemnation of you hadn't been so much a personal attack, as it was a business action. He worried his income might diminish. After all, with you in the picture, many of his followers could very well leave him."

Annette added, "We assured him that we have no intention to diminish his fund base. That, coupled with the IRS agreement, persuaded him to comply. Sometimes you have to do a little dance with the devil, but you never have to sell him your soul."

Phil continued, "They chose to support you. It seemed much easier than preaching from a cell block to satisfy the IRS."

Annette concluded, "Hunter's people did the homework and as Singleton goes, so goes the flock. We meet with Lund, Connery and Dancey over the next several days. The word is out that we hold all the cards. "

I was annoyed, "You mean to tell me the government knows these thieves are ripping off poor people and avoiding taxes and they do nothing about it? That's just wrong."

"Kathryn looked perplexed, "First of all, these religions neocons actually do provide services. They line their wallets but at the same time, they help people. In the long run their scams create jobs, keep some of the poor fed and off welfare and ultimately generate more tax revenue than they hide. And remember, not all religious leaders are like Singleton. Good churches sacrifice to make lives a bit easier. But they all need funds to help the homeless, feed the hungry and carry on their ministries."

She moved to the bed, picked up her purse from the floor and rummaged through as she spoke, "Churches ask for donations. People give money and end up feeling good about their sacrifice. Some give to assure a spot in Heaven but, whatever their beliefs, if it works for them, it's not up to us to judge."

"When the scam artists blatantly piss the money away, they eventually get caught. It's just a matter of time" She zipped her purse and threw it to the floor. "Does anyone have a cigarette?" She looked to each of us and one by one we all shook our heads. "Good, I quit last week."

She continued, "Jeremy, we didn't make the laws but we can use them for a greater good. Once you're established, speak out against anything or anyone you choose, but until then we need the support."

Annette spoke, "Studies indicate donations across the board should rise with the advent of your presence. It'll have the same effect as the Tsunami and the hurricanes; more awareness, more donations, more for everyone. Oral Roberts gave candles and told people there was no need to send money. It plucked at heart strings and donations poured in. We don't have to ask. It's a byproduct. Money will come."

"And if it does, I'll ship it right back."

"Wait a moment, Jeremy. Realize what you're saying." Kathryn came to me, placed both hands on my shoulders and looked directly into my eyes. "You will be a central figure, in not only this country, but the world. People will offer support in any way they can. You won't become another Singleton. We won't squander money on personal gain. It'll all go to good purpose. You have the opportunity to do what no one else has ever done."

Her hands moved from my shoulders and encircled me. She spoke into my ear, "You can choose to travel the country on foot and live off people along the way. You won't get very far. You're international and you need to reach as many as you can while the opportunity exists. It's in motion. You can't quit and you can't go back to Ann Arbor. They won't let you. Accept the fact that people will give you money."

Beyond Kathryn's smoky voice was a faint ringing in my ears. I pulled away, moved to a dining chair and fell onto it. The familiar emptiness that had become my existence these past weeks lifted its dagger and stabbed me again.

She was right, nothing I could do would make this go away. My fate was set and I could only hope it wouldn't be the same as my predecessor. I sat and listened to a murmur in the background about the hour. Finally, Kathryn leaned over and said, "Get some rest, Jeremy. We've got a lot ahead of us and we all need to rejuvenate. Things will be brighter in the morning."

She hugged me. I shook hands with Phil and Annette and as the door closed behind them, I was suddenly more alone than I'd ever been in my life.

I needed a distraction, a magazine, a list of local events, anything. My suitcase lay on a stand in the corner. The edge of an envelope was visible, the one passed to me by the nurse at the hospital. It was still unopened and addressed, simply to 'Jeremy'. I picked it up, studied it a few moments, slipped my finger under the flap and tore it open.

I pulled out what seemed a thick letter, but when I unfolded the paper, it was stuffed with hundred dollar bills. They dropped to the floor and lay at my feet. I looked around to see if there was anyone watching. I was alone.

The page contained a short note written by a shaky hand. It said, "Better it goes to you than the mortician. You gave me back my life, God bless you." Under that, it was signed, "Avery Carlson".

I retrieved the bills from the floor and returned them and the note to the envelope. I made the decision to personally return the money to Avery Carlson as soon as I could. No one would have it but him.

I placed the envelope in my coat pocket and went to bed.

THIRTY FOUR

My outlook softened after a night's sleep. The sun broke over the horizon. The soft, buttery light of fall glowed in my windows to warm me and my feelings for the team. I finally agreed to work with them and the next two days became a study of who I'd become and preparation for what I might be. The hours became a constant series of ideas, discussions, arguments, heated arguments, compromise and yet more arguments. In the end we agreed upon general localities, time frames, agendas, items for discovery, statements to avoid at all cost and of course, the message. Virtually every facet of the coming three months of my life were plotted and defined.

One ongoing major disagreement involved my demands that we confront Washington about the president's possible liability for The Cape. Congressional investigations had slogged down after the Evans assignation. Although things were moving forward, there was a huge gap in the system so momentum was dragging along slowly. The team was firm that I should spend my energy creating a future rather than attempting to define the wrongs of the past. I was to offer the 'way forward'.

Kathryn inhaled from a cigarette and released the smoke slowly as a balm for her anxiety.

I waved the smoke away, "Where'd that come from? I thought you quit."

She turned her head to the side, made a loud huffing sound and dropped the butt in a cup of cold coffee. The sizzle was muffled as she continued, "A few fragments of this government are giving you the ability to do great things if you only agree to move forward and improve the future. They want you, no, they need you to heal the rift that's been created here and around the globe."

She continued, "Jeremy, you could have been labeled a threat and taken to Guantanamo. You'd never have seen daylight again. It could have been much worse. Instead they recognized the possible benefits we offer and supported us. It might not be everything, but we need to work with the hand we've been given. We're on the moral high ground here and we can't jeopardize their assistance. We'll do far more if we move forward and work to prevent any new atrocities."

She took a pack of Marlboros from her purse and threw them in the waste can. "By the way, I did quit, but you're not making it easy."

Phil added quietly, "Washington hopes we'll be able to soften world tension. You're nearly universal now. They believe you have the capacity to unite nations and possibly bring a semblance of peace to people all over. Think about it. You can't allow your personal feelings about what's already happened interfere with what you might be capable of universally. You've got to consider the global impact. If we spend our energy digging into the dark side of our own government we'll drag the rest of the world there with us. Let Congress do the dirty work and dredge up muck. We need to stay focused on the bigger picture, on a positive future for everyone."

I laid on the bed and closed my eyes. Though I didn't want to forget the Cape and all the friends I'd lost, their arguments had relevance. I was beginning to understand the impact we might have if I focused on the future. But in the back of my mind I wondered if I might somehow be experiencing some form of the Stockholm syndrome.

Kathryn sat on the bed next to me and swept the back of her finger nails gently up and down my arm. I was absorbed by her scent and my feelings for her flooded back. I shook my head and finally conceded to their wishes. Across the room, Annette took a breath, picked up the phone and ordered dinner while I took Kathryn's hand.

THIRTY FIVE

Early the following morning, in great need of fresh air and an escape from the beige walls, I dressed, pulled on boots and a coat and stepped from the stale room into the morning chill. Stiff from far too much time in beds and chairs I needed to stretch my legs. I was sure the others were still asleep so I locked the door and began to walk. My breath became a silver fog in the gray Iowa haze.

I walked a gravel road along the parking lot that headed away from the highway until I came upon a dirt path that lead east toward a stand of trees. It seemed inviting so I decided to follow it. Several minutes later I found a small creek and the path turned and trailed along its bank. After a short while, I sat beside the water to rest, watched the current move fallen leaves downstream and wondered where they might end up, or if indeed there was an end.

The absurdity of it all made me chuckle. "This is how it's done now? A public relations team to map the morals of the savior? Maybe that's actually who the disciples were; just a P.R. team." I laughed aloud, "My God, they nearly have *me* believing it. Savior! How the hell can I save people?" I pulled my knees up and rested my head on them, curled like an upright fetus. The sound of the brook soothed me and I began to finally, truly relax for the first time in weeks. I took deep breaths and the icy air cleansed my lungs, but try as I may, I couldn't stop thoughts of the disaster from returning.

It was as though I was standing back on the stage in DC, surrounded by the lights again. My muscles spontaneously tightened to stone. I took another breath of Iowa air and attempted to relax again but the flashes continued in my memory. They'd brightened the stage all morning, soft and yellow from cameras. Throughout the audience they came, randomly, warming.

Suddenly, from my right, a series of different flashes, sharp and white hot. First one, then several in succession, without pause. The images slowed as I relived them, breathing heavily. I freed the memories and allowed them to return.

Senator Evans jumped backward, feet off the floor, a look of confusion on his face. I don't believe he even realized what had happened. People around me began tumbling over, flailing as they fell. Others turned to run and flew toward the back of the stage, falling, dying. All of them dying.

Sounds emerged to intensify the memories. Muffled pops and what seemed to be bees buzzing by. Then screams overcame everything and the air was thick with vibrations.

I'd frozen, tried to move, but my body wouldn't comply. I watched as chairs became animated, phantom holes appeared across the stage. I stood there frozen and stared helpless, at the crowd.

Richard and Maggie were driven away from me as I looked on. I was the only one left, alone. In front of me, the assassin seemed pummeled by invisible hammers from every direction. He fell from the top of a truck, this time in slow motion. The shooting had all but ceased. I heard a final pop before I collapsed to the stage. It was slick with blood.

The crowd became panic-stricken, fighting, crawling across one another to escape, grinding one another to the ground. Pandemonium forced my shock to crumble and release me. I pulled myself up with a microphone stand in time to see thousands of people rushing in every direction. What seemed a huge fishhook ripped my side to pull me back down. I gasped in pain and I tried to understand what was tearing me open but found nothing but warm dampness. There, supported by the stand, the warm glow surround me again as I viewed the chaos.

Something had to be done to calm the confusion, assure them the danger was over. My voice was a whisper but it seemed to echo from everywhere as I spoke. People froze and looked at me. Yellow flashes warmed me again. They melded into one light and the memories faded into it. I remember, someone touched me from behind, then another from the side. The crowd became quiet again. As I rose from the stage in the arms of my rescuers the memories faded.

On the bank of the brook, in the soft light, a thousand miles from that day, I wept. I cried for my friends who had died, for all the many losses and because I was now alone. I wept because I had to deal with the aftermath of all those deaths and for the responsibilities thrust upon me.

Suddenly, there in the shadows, my soul was scratched by a fingernail from hell. The shots, the white flashes from the assassin had all missed me. Of that I am sure. He died before I fell to the stage. All the remaining shots were fired at him, away from me.

It came to me as sharp as any bullet. The impact! The pop from the gun! They had come after Klein had been killed. I clenched my eyes to experience the final scene once more. The first retorts, the massive volley from the Guard, then the final shot. I remembered the impact just before I fell to the stage.

As though it were an instant replay, I repeated the scene again and this time attempted to observe every detail in slow motion. I could almost count the number of shots. They were rapid but singular at first, then began to overlap as their numbers and intensity grew.

I watched the stage come up as I started to fall and then looked back to the crowd as it boiled in every direction.

There, near some bleachers, to my left, was a man staring intently at me. He seemed oblivious to everything surrounding him. I briefly noticed him as I looked to the Guardsmen moving toward Klein, pushing through the confusion.

I replayed once more to see the man watching me. He seemed calm, unaffected, absolutely without emotion. There was a coat over his arm although the day was warm. His arm was pointed toward me and he had a detached composure that was terrifying. I could see his eyes staring directly at me. I'll never forget that face. The face of the man…who…shot…me!

I opened my eyes to the gray Iowa morning. My blood chilled to air temperature. I felt surrounded by specters, all staring at me from the trees. I had to get to some sort of safety and tell someone. I discovered the energy to bolt but as I jumped to my feet, I slipped into the brook and fell on the muddy bank. The water was ice and shocked the panic away. I found balance, rose from the mud and retraced my path. Realization that another assassin might still be out there, still after me, compelled an immediate return to the motel. I ducked and tried to move in silence as I searched the way and listened for any sign of the killer.

Back at the motel, I leaned against my room door and tried to catch my breath. The metallic taste of adrenalin was strong and my side throbbed horribly. I fished in my pocket for the room card but as I pulled it out, a car suddenly rushed into a parking spot beside me. I fumbled and watched the plastic float to the sidewalk. I pressed against the door, eyes closed, and prepared for the worse.

Car doors opened and a couple emerged, laughing. I finally looked and watched them go to another room. They both looked concerned as they passed so I offered a weak smile and retrieved my key. The man nodded as our eyes met though he seemed quite uncomfortable. I returned his nod and unlocked my door.

Inside, I collapsed on the bed, quaking with fear. I tried to calm my aching side and fired nerves. "Get a hold of yourself!" I demanded, remembering my team and the government support. "You're safe. No one even knows I'm here. They'll find this guy. I'll have a drawing made. They'll find him. He can't get to me, not anymore."

I sat up, reached for the phone and dialed Kathryn's room. After several rings and voice mail, I hung up and melted into the bed.

THIRTY SIX

A knock at the door shocked me awake. Eyes wide, I swallowed and took a deep breath. Knocking continued. "What!" I shouted from the bed. I couldn't bring myself to move from under the covers. I glanced at the clock, not more than an hour had passed since I'd returned. The only response to my question was another series of fist pounds on the door. I rose, hesitated, then moved forward, "What!" I asked again and realized that my shouts were coming as a mere whisper.

I leaned to the peep hole expecting the man with the coat about to kick his way in. Instead, standing patiently was a frail dark woman in a housekeeper's uniform. She must have seen the light wane from the peep hole, "It's housekeeping," she said softly.

I opened the door slightly, "Could you come back later?" I asked.

She looked into my eyes and a smile enveloped her, "It's really you, isn't it?"

I didn't respond but as we stared at one another it was apparent she recognized me.

"I'm not here to clean your room. She smiled timidly, "I just wanted to see you. I need to talk to you, please!"

She was obviously nervous and kept glancing to her left. There seemed to be someone with her. My thought was to slam the door and lock it, wait for Kathryn to return and handle this. My heart raced. I tried to catch breath when she spoke again, "Please, Sir." she pleaded. Her brown eyes started to tear and I realized I could be in control of the situation. I stepped out hesitantly and looked around the door to see a young girl, about eighteen, who hid against the wall. She also wore a housekeeper's uniform but she was taller than me and lanky. She was snow pale next to her friend. She held her head low and looked only at my feet.

"This is Laura, Sir. I tole her it was you here. They said I was crazy but I knew."

The entire scene was extremely awkward. I wanted them to leave but I had no idea how to ask them go without sounding like a prick. The three of us stood in silence and smiled at one another for several seconds. Across the parking lot, the door to the office opened and another employee looked out. The housekeeper glanced back and shouted, "It's him, you know I was right."

Two others came from the office. As they crossed the lot, a car stopped to let them pass. One leaned to the window and said something to the driver. The car pulled into a parking space and a man in brown got out and hurried to join the others. As they came toward my room, he spoke on a cell phone.

Within moments a few more cars turned into the lot and others began to join those surrounding me. I stood in the doorway and faced a crowd of nearly 20. They all stared in silence as though they expected me to perform a song and dance. I had no idea what to say, what to do. People whispered to one another and smiled. Heads shook as the murmur grew. I wanted it to end but just stood alone and felt foolish. I'd forced a panicked smile but it finally began to fade so I decided it was time to just step inside and close the door.

As I turned, a voice from somewhere simply said, "Do something." The crowd released a nervous chuckle. I felt I'd better respond before someone got ugly.

"What would you have me do?" I asked. At last it had started. I was absolutely alone and fought back panic.

"Do a miracle." came a woman's voice. The crowd looked at one another then back at me, waiting for a response.

"Heal someone" another shouted.

I looked at the faces, "Is someone here sick?" I looked around but there was no reply. I shrugged. Some of the smiles faded and one very large man with a beard looked angry. He began to breath hard as though he were about to say something. I realized I had to respond before the situation got out of control. Through my fear, I began, "As you might know my name is Jeremy Clay. There've been a lot of things said about me; that I have performed miracles, that I have healed people that I saved several thousand people in Washington DC."

The man who verged on anger listened intently. All eyes were fixed on me. For the first time I began to understand the power I could wield, at least until I made a fool of myself. I decided to let the crowd talk. "Do any of you have questions?"

The Woman who originally knocked on my door began to raise her hand but looked around, noticed she was alone in her action and quickly lowered it.

The crowd began to murmur again when a voice spoke just above the din, "I certainly have my doubts you're anything more than a show."

Eyes returned to me. It was comforting that someone felt like I did. "Good for you," I encouraged, "What's your name?"

"I don't need to tell you my name. If you're really the messiah you'd know it."

Silence hung in the air like icicles. No one breathed.

"Valid point," I returned, "or it would be if I was psychic, but I'm not, I'm a man, like you. The difference lies in the circumstances. I've been drawn into situations beyond comprehension, yours or mine. I have been involved in things I can't begin to explain. Things happened that are outside my conscious actions and several of those events have gained world attention. "

All faces were watching me. Many seemed to accept what I said. "What I do know, is that many people claim to be the voice of God. They believe they know what the rest of the world should do. As yet, none of them have proven their claims by word or deed. I claim no such thing and yet, my deeds seem to prove otherwise."

I raised my hands dramatically in a 'stop' gesture, "Let me assure you. I don't want your money. I don't want your possessions, I don't want any of your physical world.

"What I want is an end to killing and madness, an end to hatred."

I gazed around the crowd, "I want each of you to go to your homes this evening and resolve to do one thing to help bring about peace in our time. You don't need to dedicate all you have or promise a lifetime obligation, just decide to do one thing that will change the world for the better. Just one."

"If you do that you'll please your God, you'll help our world and you might save your own souls. That's all I ask from each of you.

"And truly Mitchel, if we do these things together, we can create something that matters, throughout this world."

The gentleman who made the statement nodded and as he did his face reddened with the realization I'd said a name and apparently it was his.

"Don't ever be afraid to doubt. Always look very deeply for the truth."

I turned to enter my room and from behind, several hands reached to touch my back. I closed the door, went to the bed and collapsed.

THIRTY SEVEN

Time passed and the crowd outside my room grew. I feel like a prisoner and all the walls seemed to close in. I was overwhelmed by claustrophobia and began to pace like a caged animal. As bad as it was, I couldn't consider facing the gathering outside. I switched on the television and changed channels incessantly for distraction. The noise masked the sounds from outside but I couldn't focus on any one program. I switched off the TV, turned on the radio and scanned through every station. There was nothing but irritating static from a tinny speaker so I turned the radio off and tried the television again hope against hope something worthwhile might have started in the past few minutes. There was nothing but tedious rubbish, but each time I turned it off the voices outside grew louder.

After nearly an hour of pacing, someone knocked. I froze mid step and hoped the mob wasn't about to demand another performance.

"Jeremy. Are you in there?" It was Kathryn. I went to the peep hole and looked out. She huddled next to the door surrounded. I undid the lock and created a small space she could slide through. The sound of voices increased exceedingly so I slammed the door behind her and bolted it.

"What the hell is going on here?" She pointed her thumb over her shoulder, and seemed to imply I had done something.

"That's what you wanted. Those are my followers, and guess what? They're following me."

She pulled the curtain back slightly and looked at the growing crowd, then dropped it and threw her briefcase on the dresser, "I stopped by this morning to take you to a meeting with one of Hunter's people but you were gone. You scared the shit out of me. They flew in from Washington last night to meet you. I told them your wound was acting up and rescheduled for this afternoon then came back here to find you. I couldn't very well tell them you were missing. I've been worried sick."

She was furious, "You disappear into nowhere and then I find a riot at your door. Don't do this to me, damn it."

"I went out for a few minutes to get a breath of air. I didn't talk to anyone, I didn't even see anyone. When I got back they knocked on the door. What can I say, they found me. I've been trapped here for more than an hour with a crowd getting bigger by the minute. I didn't invite them here, they came from nowhere."

She sighed, paced the room and chewed her thumb nail, "I'm sorry. We thought this place was isolated enough to give you some privacy. I guess we can't hide any longer. We'll need to move forward. That's what the meeting was about, your next introduction to the masses. I should have mentioned it last night but I wanted you to get some sleep."

"If I'd known, none of this would have happened." I waved my hand toward the door, "Kathryn, you have to keep me informed. I've got more at stake here than anyone."

The memories of the shooter rushed back. "Kathryn, I have to tell you…."

A thud outside cut me off. We both turned toward the door and waited. When all was quiet again, she spoke, "We have your first public appearance scheduled. I wanted you to…."

"Apparently not the first." I interrupted.

"be there to dis….." She stopped mid-sentence as my statement registered. "What's that mean, 'not the first'"?

"I had my first public presentation an hour ago. It was terrifying and a bit exciting at the same time. You won't believe it but I knew some guy's..."

"What the hell. What did you say?" She seemed concerned and fearful I'd done something destructive.

"Dammit Kathryn, I had no choice. I was surrounded by all these people and they wanted something. Was I supposed to spit on them and slam the door? What do you think the press would do with that? They all have camera phones out there. If you want me to be this person you're going to have to trust me, too. I won't have the luxury of speech writers all the time. I know what shouldn't be said. If something comes up that I can't handle, I won't fake it, I'll pass."

She didn't hear a word I said. She repeated, "What did you tell them?"

I tried to remember but it was all a blur. "I did fine, Kathryn, it was all good. It came out and they were satisfied. I left them with some thoughts and made a decent break. One thing I do remember is that some guy thought I should know his name. Near the end, it came to me and I called him by it. I believe I was right. It seemed to shock the hell out of him."

A look of wonder came over her and she began to calm. My revelation about knowing a stranger's name gave her cause to consider. She sat on the bed and stared at the ceiling.

Memories from the morning flooded back, "Listen, I have to tell you something extremely important." Her concern returned.

"There was another assassin in DC. I remembered another

gunman. The one who shot me. Not Klein, another shooter."

I had her attention, "Are you sure? Are you certain this is a memory and not your imagination?"

"I saw him, Kathryn! He was there in front of me, to the left by some bleachers. Klein was already down when this guy shot me.

"Jeremy, why didn't you mention this before? Why didn't you tell me something this important?"

"It just came back this morning. I saw him, Kathryn. I remember his face, his eyes. He was there, he tried to kill me."

She looked into my eyes for what seemed like several minutes. Suddenly she went to her purse and pulled out a card and her cell phone.

"Who are you calling?"

She finished dialing and put the phone to her ear as she spoke to me, "The FBI. They need to know about...Yes. David Fulton please. Sure. Kathryn Lawson ..." She lowered the phone, "They need to know there's still a threat...Yes... Please have him get back to me as soon as possible. It's extremely urgent. He has my number. Thank you." she pushed a button and put the phone away.

"If there was another shooter..."

I was shocked, "What do you mean if…."

Kathryn closed her eyes and raised her hands to the sides of her face in a stop motion, "I'm simply saying that we can find out who he was." She lowered her hands and looked at me wide eyed, "We'll be alright, Jeremy. We'll get to the bottom of all this." She clenched her hands and continued, "You're absolutely sure there was someone else? This isn't just one of those stress situations where people imagine memories?"

I could feel my face redden as I glared at her. Before I could say anything she continued, "O.K., O.K. I believe you, Let's not panic. No need to panic. As soon as we pass this on they'll be on top of it. They'll take care of it before you know it."

There was a thump at the door. I jumped and backed up as the handle wiggled. The crowd was getting restless. Voices were suddenly louder. "It looks like it's time to move on," Kathryn sounded concerned as she looked at the door.

I fell into the chair and closed my eyes. Staring back through the darkness was the man with the coat over his arm, eyes like ice, no emotion. I saw a flash come through the coat and all the while, those fucking eyes never blinked.

THIRTY EIGHT

The library in Woodward, Iowa was our first stop in a random Midwestern tour. The team wanted to introduce me to limited numbers in more remote areas that had minor proximity to the media. The idea was to speak with smaller groups and refine our message from the responses. We wanted to limit access to papers and TV. There was no announcement of our itinerary. Our schedule was confidential with small venues reserved in various staff names. With only 1,200 people in Woodward we expected to draw a crowd of no more than 50 or 60. Our presentation was scheduled for noon on the second day after our arrival and information was only made available to local businesses the morning of my talk.

Our team spent the entire day before and the morning of the event questioning me to help prepare. There were numerous suggestions about possible interpretations of my answers. I had to break on several occasions to try and absorb as much information as I could. It was overwhelming but Kathryn constantly assured me it would become easier as we went forward. The wonderful thing was that throughout all the thousands of possible statements and responses we discussed, I was given final say on what my comments would consist of.

As I prepared to move to the library I felt ill. On top of facing fifty or sixty strangers and attempting to convince them I was who people suggested, the fear of the man with the coat on his arm continued to plague me. I wondered if I could actually get through this. A scripted press conference and twenty people outside a motel room had both been terrifying, although they had gone rather smoothly, but a planned speech to a larger group was stupefying.

A knock at my door meant it was to begin. My heart sank at the thought of driving to the library. Phillip entered with a reassuring smile. "Jeremy, great news." He came close and put his hand on my shoulder. "We had a call from Hunter's office about a second shooter." He patted me as I stiffened, "They said the FBI reviewed all of the photos and available videos they could get their hands on. They studied them in detail. They was no indication of another gunman." He stepped back and continued, "They found your man with the coat. He was checked and he's clean. It was only a coat. They said it was most probably a glare from a cell phone, but not a gun. We've been assured." He reached for the door and smiled back, "No threat. We're good to go. Let's meet our public."

I stood in shock. All my preparation followed Phillip through the door. I looked at Kathryn and saw her hollow smile as she came to me. "It'll be alright, Jeremy. We won't stop looking. I'll have our people find out who the man was and we'll check into it personally. I believe you saw something. We won't stop until we find out what it was. I'm sorry, but you can be sure we'll do what it takes to resolve this."

Our van pulled behind the Library to a packed lot. Cars were everywhere and there wasn't space to stop, let alone park. We were ushered through a rear door. As I entered the main room it was empty and I heard myself sigh heavily. I thought, 'a reprieve'. However, our hosts were ecstatic and the air crackled with excitement as they lead me through the building to the front. The door opened and before the building stood a crowd of nearly 1,200 people. I froze mid-step as I finally faced reality. I had to address a massive crowd. I scanned the area for anyone with a coat on their arm but in the brisk Iowa afternoon everyone had coats. I felt Kathryn's hand on my back and she whispered in my ear, "This is it. We're all here with you."

I heard my name and applause filled the town. I walked to the microphone and waited for the noise to subside. As the clapping faded I could hear my heart pounding in my ears. I just hoped to remain conscious. Suddenly there was silence. No one seemed to breathe and I wondered if they could hear my heart throbbing. I cleared my throat and a grotesque sound rang from the speakers and accosted me. I forgot everything and stood in silence, all the while my heart pumped harder and louder. My mind screamed for something to say, something we had discussed but all I could do was look at the faces and wonder which one wanted to shoot me.

Tension covered me like honey, slow and thick. It became difficult to breath and I believed the end had come. All the headlines, all the public relations, all the preparation were about to end as I stood frozen and alone.

A voice came from somewhere in the gathering. I didn't see who spoke, I just knew it sounded extremely threatening, "What gives you the right to say you're Christ?"

My mind raced as I stood there, totally void. I tried to imagine the thousands of scenarios we had discussed. I searched in vain for a nonexistent teleprompter. I'd been coached with tens of thousands of responses, but my mind was an empty box. There was nothing. I wanted to run but my legs wouldn't cooperate. I felt like a target at a shooting range. The people began to roil, quietly at first but their sounds grew.

I turned my head to look for help and I saw Kathryn stepping forward with fear in her eyes and suddenly I was surrounded by a warmth that I couldn't explain. My heart beat slowed and my breath began to regulate. I raised my hand to her and smiled. When I turned to the tensioning throng they took on a hazy, yellow cast. I realized I was speaking to the microphone but although the voice from the speakers was familiar it wasn't mine. It sounded the same as the one that spoke in DC. It was distant and serene, and although I was actually talking, the sound was from someone else and was utterly soothing.

The voice said, "I'll answer your question with a story. Several people came upon an odd creature while walking in a forest. They gathered around this thing as it lay on the forest floor, curled in a moist ball. They'd never seen anything quite like it and wondered what it might be."

"After a time, the creature began to move. The people watched intently, each trying to make sense of it as it slowly emerged from its position and stood on two feet. It unfolded its arms and stretched them to the warm breeze."

"The arms ended without hands and as the breeze flowed around them, the crowd realized they were covered by fine downy feathers. 'They must be wings,' said one. "It's a bird,' said another."

"They all agreed the creature had to be a bird. One by one they asked the creature 'if you're a bird, tell us what kind of bird you are."

"The creature looked around and replied, 'I've made no claim to be who any of you say I am. I am but the truth you see before you. Believe of me what you will, it's a choice unto you. Should your belief bring you joy or pain, that too is a choice. You have free will. I am here as I am, not to prove myself to you but just to be. Each of you must choose what you believe."

"With that the creature raised its wings to the wind and flew away."

I looked into the heart of the gathering and continued, "It's up to you to decide your truth. You can accept or deny anything you see. Find comfort, find joy, live in peace or reject, hate and condemn. You make the world you live in."

For more than an hour I answered questions about creating one's own reality and bliss, to the satisfaction of the crowd. When it came time to leave, several hundred more people had arrived. As I returned to the library, there was no applause, just a warm silence.

The team met me inside the building. Kathryn threw her arms around me and cried with joy. We stood surrounded by our people, everyone patting me on the back and arms.

As they all touched me. Kathryn's cheek was next to mine and she whispered, "Jeremy, I believe in you."

THIRTY NINE

We presented in seven towns through the Midwest without announcement and each time the crowds grew larger. When we reached Winchester, Ohio the entire county was immobilized. A decision was made to move West, continue working the smaller cities and build toward Los Angeles.

Throughout our initial appearances the media had a somewhat curious 'wait and see' attitude. Those who were most critical the first days revised their stories within hours of their original critiques. I could only imagine the evangelical steamroller of Reverend Singleton had something to do with those changes of heart. The right Reverend's fear of the IRS was apparently far more developed than his disdain for me.

The entire week, local news anchors reported on and interviewed hundreds of people who claimed to have been healed after visiting one of my presentations. People spoke of lives being saved, futures preserved and overwhelming hope enveloping them. I could understand some sort of political pressure influencing the religious spokespeople but nothing could explain how the average person became convinced to pass these glowing assessments. Each time I questioned Kathryn, she shook her head and smiled as though it would be beyond my capacity to understand, even if she could explain.

Two days later we flew into Spokane International Airport in route to Ritsville, Washington. Our destination was confidential and the information tightly guarded. Reservations were made last minute, however, when we arrived at Spokane, the airport was mobbed with throngs of followers. Arrangements had been made from the air for transportation but word had somehow gotten out. The drive down 395 was nearly stop and go. A pack of cars followed us and hundreds of people parked on the side of the highway as we passed. We checked into our rooms through a wall of security. The dynamics of our program were becoming impossible.

At a press conference that afternoon I recognized some of the faces. They were no longer local, small town talking heads. Far more familiar news people were there to report. Even though the principals were better known, their questions were all still fairly standard. TV news featured us daily, both nationally and internationally. I imagined the interest and my glory would soon begin to wane. My celebrity would start to fade as soon as there was nothing new to report. My fifteen minutes were ticking and it felt as though there could actually be a light at the end of this media tunnel.

I believe the team felt it too. There were discussions about moving into the major venues a bit sooner and grabbing as much of the spotlight as we could as quickly as possible. There were calls I wasn't included in, to people whom I could only imagine were at the reins of the project. Each time these specific calls were made or received either I or the person on the phone was shuffled to another room behind closed doors. Kathryn continuously explained the subject was scheduling. They wanted to keep information private to quell leaks that seemed to precede us. It was apparent by the way she held her pen like a cigarette and kept attempting to take a drag that there was more to the calls than she let on. Her nerves betrayed the fact that she wasn't being totally honest.

Our presentation was scheduled for seven that evening at an old railroad station that had been converted to a community play house. At five I was shuttled to the site and escorted through the already growing crowds to become familiar with the venue. On the stage, speaking to a group of reporters was a gentleman who owned an air transport company from Eastern Washington. I was asked to join him. When we were introduced he shook my hand vigorously.

"It's my absolute pleasure to have this opportunity to meet you Mr. Clay." He beamed toward the cameras, "After becoming engulfed in the crowds and confusion at the airport this morning I knew it was my duty to make your travels more convenient and facilitate you in bringing your message to the world. Tonight, I would be honored to offer you and your entourage one of Lehland's helicopters for your continuing travels throughout the West Coast. I would also be delighted to offer my personal services as your pilot in this historic event."

With that he handed me a symbolic set of keys to the helicopter as the warm flashes from cameras filled the house. I thanked him and accepted his gift.

An announcer stepped to the microphone and whipped up the audience as he clapped and shouted, "Robert Lehland folks, let's hear it for Robert Lehland and Lehland Transportation, one of Ritzville's favorite sons." The crowd cheered and I felt I was in the heart of an infomercial.

Later, after introductions, I opened questions to the overflowing audience and worked with them for nearly two hours, answering doubts, softening fears and providing solace to the masses. When we were done, a series of collection bags began to move forward. I stepped back to the stage and asked the followers to keep their money. I explained that any funds that had already been donated would be left for community charities. I then exited the stage.

Later that evening as the crowds diminished, we made our way to the van to return to our motel. As the driver turned onto Division, we witnessed a huge demonstration and drove slowly past the crowds. I realized they were two factions about to collide. My supporters were in a line shouting at several others who carried signs accusing me of being the anti-Christ. The groups screamed and began to push one another. Sheriff cars were parked in a nearby lot but the deputies seemed to be waiting for back up. They were greatly outnumbered. Our security demanded the driver move out ASAP. As we lurched forward I shouted, "Stop the van!"

"Jeremy?" Kathryn began to panic. "Driver…"

Someone shouted "Move out, NOW!"

"Stop the van," I demanded, "I can't let this happen. This is about me." The van halted and I pulled the sliding door. As I stepped from the vehicle a few demonstrators recognized me and started my way. The front lines were engaged in their shouting/pushing match and didn't immediately notice the change of focus. As I stepped forward several people touched me and much of the noise began to fade.

One of the opposition looked up as I approached. He turned from the man he was screaming at. The hate on his face intensified when he recognized me and he pushed his adversary to the ground. He screamed, "Satan!" and threw his picket sign to the side. The words stung my ears both from volume and intent. I stood silent and watched him approach. Kathryn and the others implored me to come back. From the corner of my eye I noticed a deputy draw his gun and move toward us. The man who had been pushed down, rose and jumped on the back of his assailant. Others joined in, the mob began to boil and I saw the remaining deputy take a stance, his gun leveled on the melee. Signs began to flail, people pushed and I heard the sound of fists pounding bones. A hand grabbed my arm and pulled me back. I looked in the eyes of one of my security people, pulled loose and moved into the hostility. Madness surrounded me as people pummeled one another. The odd thing was that although the hatred and support were centered on me, it was as though I were invisible. The fight raged around me but didn't seem to include me. A woman to my left was knocked to the ground and from somewhere, a heavy boot kicked her face. Blood gushed from her nose. She flailed what was left of her picket sign as she attempted to beat people away. I knelt down to help and received the edge of her stick on my left wrist. The stick snapped in two and it felt as though my forearm might have shattered with it.

I reached for her and she stopped flailing. She looked at me and her eyes widened with fear. She cringed as though I were about to wield my wrath on her. When I touched her she calmed. I wrapped her in my arms and stood up from the asphalt. As we rose together in the black heart of enmity, the strange warmth visited upon me again. We stood together, blood from her face dripping on my shirt, her head rested on my chest.

A few around us stopped fighting and stared. Some were pummeled from behind but they didn't respond. They stood, oblivious to the hits and watched. Within moments calm proliferated through the entire mob and as quickly as it had begun, the war was over. All eyes were on me and I realized tears were streaming down my face. The woman raised her head and looked at me. Tears immediately flowed from her eyes, washing blood from her cheeks and chin. I helped her stand and she stumbled back from me. A man in western garb with a huge beard rushed to her side and heaved sobs as he hugged her. She buried her face in his shirt and they retreated into the crowd.

I looked at the mob surrounding me and whispered, "What have you done?"

Some seemed embarrassed, some looked away. Others were still angry.

"Don't fight each other in my name. Disagree if you will but never hurt another for me. Those of you who feel I'm here to debase your beliefs, please read the words of Christ. Don't dare corrupt His teachings."

One man turned, retrieved a protest sign and held it high. He was still filled with hate.

"Today I give you, and everyone who hears this, a new commandment. From this point forward, the name of God, whatever that may be to you, will no longer be used as an excuse for fighting and hatred. If you choose to hurt another on this earth, you do so of your own accord and you will be held personally accountable in the end."

I turned to the van and people parted as I passed. When we drove off I noticed the man who was angry. He looked around for support and when he found none, he lowered his sign and walked away.

FORTY

We flew fairly low above the Columbia, north and west of Portland and arrived in Dundee, Oregon without incident. I was surprised at the size of the helicopter Lehland had provided. I thought it would be similar to a news chopper, noisy and cramped. However, he escorted us in an executive craft. I never even considered if it were part of his fleet or somehow donated for our use by the powers behind my fame.

We landed in an open area of a local vineyard and were transported by limousine to their winery for lodging. Since it was private property there were no followers other than invited guests. It was refreshing to have alone time after more than a week of notoriety. We were treated to a wonderful lunch combined with small talk. The guests had been asked to respect my space but I agreed to pose for photos after the meal to thank them and so, was allowed a quiet night in a suite with a plush bed and a hot tub.

***

The following day we prepared for our presentation while I

read the headlines of a newspaper that described occurrences in Ritzville. They again included information that had been enhanced and embellished to include miracles and things that never actually took place. Although there were hundreds of witnesses, people who were interviewed each attested to the exaggerations. I was beginning to wonder if people were somehow involved in a mass hysteria.

A footnote to the story referred to the investigation behind the missing nuclear material used in the Cape Sardis bomb. Information had apparently been exposed that suggested a high ranking member of Interglobal Aeronautics and former diplomatic representative to Saudi Arabia was being examined. Speculation was that the terrorists had been recruited for reasons other than revenge, one of those being the acquisition of major military contracts. I was livid at the possibility that thousands had died for monetary gain and even the IMP might have been manipulated by corporate greed.

That evening, we traveled by van to our presentation at Dundee High School. We again needed escorts into the building two hours prior to the start, due to the crowds. When the doors finally opened, the mass moved in and filled the gymnasium. The area surrounding the school was gridlocked by onlookers. I wondered if we would need the helicopter just to leave.

I was introduced to an auditorium with standing room only and immediately opened the floor to questions. I wanted to distract the crowd from claustrophobia. The technique had become a dependable approach to engage the audience and allowed common concerns to be addressed up front. I was able to quell most fears before discussing the prescribed agenda.

This time however, there were several questions pertaining to statements I'd made in the Ritzville parking lot.

There were requests for clarification about my stand on fighting and defense. Rather than the planned agenda, I spoke to the fallacy of war in the name of religion; an eye for an eye and the context in which it had been used in the New Testament.

I was asked how my comments applied to the military with questions like, "Do you suggest we allow terrorists to attack us? Should we allow another 911 or Cape? Are you saying the military is evil?"

I spoke to all their concerns, "At this time the threats to humanity come from humanity itself. As a people, we have not developed to a level where we can eliminate defense and it is sane and appropriate to protect ourselves, our loved ones and our neighbors. The problem has been that defense is regularly used as a synonym for offence, quite often in the name of a supreme being. Unprovoked attacks on others for any reasons are simply not acceptable, although it has been done time and time again throughout history."

Another voice rang out from the audience microphone, "Are you suggesting that when there's a threat we do nothing until someone dies?"

"I'm suggesting that to attack others because you perceive a threat is wrong. To cloak those attacks in the name of the Lord, or freedom, or liberty when actual reasons are financial or corporate is blasphemy."

"We have developed the strongest military and the most terrifying weapons on the face of the earth. We assume these arsenals deter our enemies and preserve our safety and yet we market them around the world for the sole purpose of seeing them used so we can create more. "

The crowd began to buzz. I remained silent for a few moments. "Let me suggest something with a story,

"A town was consumed with football. They wanted desperately to be successful but larger cities had all the advantages, more athletes to choose from, more money for coaching, better equipment."

"One spring, nine healthy, strong boys were born to the town. The community came together and decided all of them would contribute to the futures of those children. They agreed to focus their combined resources on these nine boys. Every family offered to forgo some essentials so they could provide time and income to train and equip these children to develop them into the best football players in the state."

"When the boys were high school age their competence was known throughout the league. As they prepared for their initial game, the state athletic commission, responding to complaints, determined these players had unfair advantage and could not participate. The boys were devastated. The families had invested all their time and fortunes preparing and equipping the team to compete."

I asked the audience, "What would you do?"

Several in the audience shouted, "Play them!"

I continued, "Indeed, that's what was done, despite the ruling and the fact all results were void."

"By the same token, we as a nation have dedicated a majority of our energy and wealth to create massive weapons and militaries. It then becomes almost ludicrous not to put those expenditures to purpose. When an economy is based on weapons and destruction, if for no other reason but to continue growing the wealth, we *will* use those resources, even when a threat never appears."

"Our nation has invested its future in weaponry and like the townspeople who were committed to their football players, we've become obligated to use those weapons. Once and for all, we need to end this commitment to war."

FORTY ONE

Our next destination was Eugene, Oregon. It was decided to move from small towns and embrace larger cities as we moved toward Los Angeles. We hoped to better understand logistics and experience much larger gatherings.

Lehland flew East and South over the Cascade Mountains so to escape the news choppers that were likely join us from Portland or Salem. The mountains were glorious. I had never seen such rugged terrain.

He finally brought us West again into a huge valley, dotted with odd hills protruding out of the flat. The interstate stretched out below with a city in the distance. As we drew closer to Eugene, Lehland pointed above us. "Here they come," he stated and shook his head. We were joined by two news helicopters that began to mimic our every move.

We were cleared to land on top of the Hult Center, downtown. Our news shadows hovered above for a bit but were forced to move on. They had no place to put down. Flak from the radio emphasized the irritation of the television crews. They argued with the Hult crew for a moment but finally flew off. I was extremely pleased with our new freedom. As we exited the copter a team from the Hult met us. I gave a large 'thumbs up' to Robert Lehland as we left and he was helped to secure his aircraft.

We were escorted to our rooms to rest prior to preparation for the following day. I placed my suitcase in the closet and dropped to the bed. It was wonderful and I wanted to stay but we were to meet in two hours so I rose and went to the bathroom to freshen up.

Through the splashing water in the sink, I heard the door open. "Kathryn?" I shouted, but there was no response.

I closed the faucets, grabbed a towel and stepped into the bedroom to find a young woman standing there. She wore a service uniform and was obviously frightened; slightly bent with her arms crossed in front of her as though protecting herself.

She didn't seem a threat but I still spoke hesitantly, "I don't need room service, please come back later." I tried to appear calm but my heart was thumping from the intrusion.

"Mr. Clay?" Her eyes were wide, her voice broken. She stepped forward and reached into a pocket.

"Please." I stammered, "I don't have time right now, I'll have to ask you..."

"Mr. Clay, I have something for you."

I started to reach toward the phone when she raised her voice, "Wait! Just a second, please. I need to give this to you."

She pulled a battered envelope from her pocket and held it out. "Just this. It's a letter addressed to you."

I looked at the envelope then back to her as she attempted a smile.

I took the letter from her trembling hand and glanced at it. It was addressed with only my name. I turned it over and on the back was a sticker stating 'E. Frasier' from Detroit.

I glared at the envelope then up at her, "Where did you get this? How…?"

She seemed confused, more frightened and stammered, "My boyfriend's cousin in Detroit sent it here. He works for a TV station and said he figured you'd be in Portland or Eugene when you left Ritzville. He asked Bobby, my boyfriend, if he could find you to give it to you. This morning they told us we had a special guest coming and I hoped it was you. Since I work here Bobby gave me this and told me to be sure you got it."

"I don't understand, why..?"

"Bobby's cousin said he found this person who knew you but she was scared to death to talk to him so he promised to keep her a secret. She said the only way she'd talk is if he got this letter to you. He told Bobbie it could mean something really big so we told him we'd try." She looked at me pleadingly, "Bobby works the green chain in Springfield. He hates it. He said this could be his ticket out."

She looked into my eyes and her face softened, "Me, I just wanted to see you. That's all. I don't want anything else." She smiled, "but instead I got to meet you."

She started to kneel down. It was an extremely uncomfortable moment. I took her arm to stop her when a noise came from the hallway. She jumped up and turned toward the door.

"I gotta' go," she said, "If they find me here I'm fired. We were told to stay away. Please don't tell anyone I was here. I just had to give you your letter."

She reached the door and searched the hallway through the peep hole. I called to her, "Wait a second." I went to the desk and wrote on the hotel pad. "If you and Bobby get a chance, show this at the door tomorrow." I handed her the note asking that they be afforded front row seats.

She read it, "Oh, thank you, thank you so much."

"On the contrary, thank you…and Bobby. I can't promise anything other than a seat to the event, but thank you for the letter."

When she exited, I double locked the door and fastened the safety chain. I fell on the bed again and held another mysterious letter in front of me. Ellen had reached out and found me again. I tried to evaluate all the alternatives. She'd never know I'd received the letter if I didn't read it. It couldn't be blackmail again. She had to realize the consequences. On the other hand, maybe she'd seen the light, maybe she hoped I could accomplish something. Maybe she'd sprouted angel wings and a halo. I laughed aloud.

If it was Ellen, it had to be bad news. She was probably lurking out there somewhere, waiting to destroy me. Something really big, indeed. I flipped the letter toward the trash.

The phone rang and brought me back to the room. I lifted the receiver to say hello, however, Kathryn was already talking, "… they want to meet at five. We need to go over everything before they arrive. I know its short notice but please be here so we can figure out a strategy."

"Who, Kathryn? Before who gets here?"

"Jeremy, please. Room 715, just down the hall. Right now, we don't have a lot of time. We'll talk when you get here."

I knocked on the door to Kathryn's room and it opened to the entire staff. I stepped in surrounded by tension. Annette took my arm and led me to chair by the window. Kathryn was speaking, "We need to present a united front before they arrive." She turned to me and spoke rapidly, "Jeremy, we need to modify your message. You infuriated several people with your speach in Dundee. The director is here with some demands."

I looked at her as though she was mad. I couldn't grasp what she was trying to say, "Director? Kathryn, what the hell are you talking about?"

She raised her voice, "Jeremy, listen to me. Your entire presence is due to the benevolence of these people. None of this has been free. You wanted to give all the money back and they allowed that. They are who pressured damn near everyone to support you. They took the IRS to Singleton. They made the deals with all the rest. They've protected us and given us nearly free reign. None of this would have been possible without them. We're indebted, big time."

I stood to leave and Phillip gently pressed me back to the chair.

"Don't do this, Jeremy. Please work with us. There's no time to argue, it's crucial we agree with him. He'll be here in fifteen minutes. They've asked us to agree with a few minor concessions. If we ease their concern they'll yield to us and we can move forward."

I attempted to rise again and a hand took my arm. I pushed it off, "Someone better explain what the hell's going on here and it better be quick. What concessions. What are you saying? You're telling me they want to control what I say?"

I looked to Kathryn, "I truly don't think that's possible at this point."

Kathryn put her fists to her forehead and clenched her eyes. Annette began to pace in front of the window. Phillip fell into the chair. Heat rose from my collar. Anger cracked in my jaw and I realized I had clenched my teeth to the point of pain.

Kathryn held her hands out and reached to me, "You have to trust me. Jeremy, we've come this far and I haven't lied to you or fucked with you once. Please, just listen. This is the critical moment in everything we've done. I know it sounds crazy but it's essential to our security, our future. Please!"

She pleaded for my help. I looked at her and my knotted muscles softened. I took a breath for the first time in several moments. "Go ahead. Tell me, I want to know."

"We've all worked our asses off to reach this point. We had to make some agreements to get the support and allow you to take the limelight." She opened her purse, rustled through it and threw it on the bed.

"In Dundee you railed against the weapons industry. That wasn't supposed to be part of the program. You winged it and it's had a major impact. Several contractors, here on the West Coast, employ thousands of people and make billions of dollars creating these military systems you so thoroughly ravaged.

"E-mails, blogs, phone calls and letters have flooded Washington demanding they stop building and financing weapons. Congress is being whipped like a dog. The only more powerful group you could have pissed off are the oil companies." She half smiled.

"Hunter himself will be here..." She looked at her watch, "in about ten minutes. He wants you to leave the military and weapons manufacturers out of your considerations."

I looked out the window at the city and rubbed my neck. "What if I tell him to go to hell? What if I continue to say what I choose to say?"

Phillip stopped pacing and shouted, "Listen. If you haven't figured this out yet, we aren't in some damn game show where you answer wrong and go home. You can't begin to imagine how much they've invested in you, in all of this." he waved his arm, "It's calculated to improve our status around the world, help our economy, heal the United States. They need you right now to repair the hatred we've inspired this past two decades."

He put his hand on the back of the chair, "But believe this, as big as you've become, they're still bigger, much bigger. They have the ability to destroy everything and crush all of us. They helped create this, they can discredit you just as fast." He snapped his fingers, "Like that, we could all just disappear. Like it or not, there are billions, if not trillions at stake and that money moves this nation.

Annett added, "There's so much we can still accomplish, so many people we can help. Just don't give them a reason to stop us. In another year it may all be over anyway, but think of what we can do in the meantime. If we just consent to this single request we can go on to realize so much, help so many."

Kathryn placed her hands on my shoulders, she had tears welling and she looked truly terrified, "Jeremy, please. Just give them this one concession. Give us a bit more time. At least wait until we've reached Los Angeles. We can go forward or let it fade by then. Don't bite the hand and destroy every possibility we have. There's so much further we can take this."

A sharp knock on the door startled everyone and we all froze.

The three looked at me with pleading eyes as Phillip went to let our "manager" in.

FORTY TWO

I couldn't sleep so I paced the room. To everyone's relief, the person at the door had been a hotel employee with a message from the "director", a simple note of positive assurance. We'd become no more than nervous pawns for someone who answered to a group of corporate executives. I'd almost begun to believe in my power and it was a more exhilarating experience than I could ever imagine. A simple gardener with virtually no impact on anything was suddenly in control of world opinion. How the hell did that happen? Now this? Those who had convinced me I could do anything and fought for me to step into the position, now demanded I follow new rules. They were terrified, both of the power I'd obtained and of those who actually ran the show. Were they simply concerned for their careers or was it truly more than that? They implied their lives might actually be in danger?

It seemed to become even more absurd and as I sat on the bed, drying from a shower, I noticed the envelope from Ellen on the floor next to the trash. I retrieved it and placed it in the pocket of the jacket that hung on the chair. What else could go wrong? Despite everything, it was beginning to seem there was always farther to fall.

Indeed, I felt it, something huge was about to happen but I couldn't grasp what it might be. I fell on the bed, closed my eyes and tried to rest but through the night, sleep wouldn't come. I tossed and turned and looked at the glow of the clock nearly every half hour.

***

A next evening, I listened from the wings of the stage as the mayor of Eugene spoke to the auditorium. It was unusually warm but my skin was clammy and sweat trickled down my side. I pulled in my arms to absorb it when I heard the envelope crinkle in my coat pocket. Now seemed as good a time as any to receive my next threat so I pulled it out and opened it. There was just a single page inside, written by an unsteady hand rather than Ellen's obnoxious swirls.

I read:

> Dear Jeremy,
>   I hope you get this. The man from channel seven said he would do his best. They say you're some kind of messenger from God. They say you do miracles. I never saw it, but if you actually can, I need one for Ellen. I have some bad news. The police were here last

night to tell me Ellen is dead. They said she set your house on fire then shot herself, committed suicide. Everything burned to the ground and they found her inside holding a gun. They say she was on drugs when she did it. Jeremy, you know Ellen didn't do drugs and she'd never shoot herself, that's just crazy. If you are everything they say you are, please find out what happened and most of all, pray for her. I don't know how she died but she shouldn't have to go to hell. Please help.

    Love, Evelyn

I couldn't absorb the words. I jumped from 'suicide' to 'burned' to 'drugs' and back again. I finally focused on 'suicide'. Ellen thought far too much of herself to take her own life. She certainly had no gun, and she refused to even build a fire in the fireplace. Drugs? She once took laughing gas at a dentist's office and complained because she'd lost control. The only thing Ellen valued more than Ellen was control. Why would she give that up?

My attention was pulled back when someone shook my shoulder. A man smiled at me and attempted to say something through the noise as applause filled the center. I couldn't hear a word.

Kathryn came to me and mouthed, "Are you O.K? I looked at her as though she were a stranger. She tried to ask me something but I couldn't hear her.

I shouted, 'You knew, didn't you?" A confused, frightened look came across her and she put her hand to her ear so I would repeat what I'd said.

I held the letter out. She took it and began to read.

"What the hell is this?" I shouted but she didn't hear me over the roar of the crowd.

I moved toward the stage, felt her hand on my shoulder pulled away and stepped forward into the spotlight. The spot followed me to the center and the crowd went wild. They screamed, whistled and chanted my name. After a few moments I raised my hands and the auditorium fell silent.

I stood quiet for a few moments while Kathryn watched from the wings in total astonishment. She tried to mouth something but I couldn't tell what she said. She seemed shocked and held out the letter to Phillip when he stepped up beside her. She shook her head back and forth slowly as though she knew what I was about to do. Phillip read the note.

I turned back toward the silent audience as the entire crowd sat on the edge of their seats, waiting. I had no idea what to say. I looked around and adrenalin suddenly surged through me. I was at once overwhelmed by a rush of power. I nearly lifted up from the stage, spoke into the microphone and simply said "Welcome".

My voice thundered from everywhere. It vibrated in my chest, I not only felt the power, I realized I *was* the power.

Before I could decide, before I even thought, the words began to flow. They didn't come from me, but through me and I refused to edit what occurred. Thoughts of Ellen lying dead, killed by another weapon of war rushed from me and into the microphone,

"I am not here to offer you salvation tonight. I'm not here to provide you health or prosperity. I'm here to remind you that the power of God cannot be given to you. It already exists within you. It allows your heart to beat, your blood to flow, your lungs to draw breath and most importantly, God's power allows you to think, decide and act. You don't need me to deliver you. Each of you has the power within,

"Some of you are doctors." Applause broke from numerous people. "Some are mill workers." Several stood, hooted and applauded.

"It doesn't matter what your place is in this world, you each have a universal power within. We all seem to have forgotten that we can and do, create anything we choose. We are currently mired in a world of war. Many say we were drawn into it, we had no choice, we can only defend our way of life. I'm here tonight to tell you that this is an absolute lie. We live in a society based on destruction. A world that develops weapons of death to support the wealth of its leaders. An economy based on murder in the name of defense."

"Each year, these leaders and their corporate supporters develop greater and more devastating weapons to stockpile and to sell to others nations so they may defend themselves against the very same weapons we've created."

"It's a cycle of madness that has caused the deaths of millions upon millions and eventually, will bring about the total annihilation of our species. For what? To make money for those few who never face the destructive power they create."

"Realize, the reason we're here today began with the devastation of an American city by hateful people. But realize this too; none of it would have been possible if our country hadn't created the means to deliver this terror in the first place. The truest terrorists are those who finance these weapons of hate, those who develop them and those who both sell and use them."

"I'm not asking that the world roll over and allow mad men to use existing arsenals against us. I am saying, here and now, we must bring an end to this economy of destruction. We must stop producing greater and more horrible methods of killing one other and stop laying waste to this world."

"People across the earth have become rich from the blood of their fellow human beings. For an economy based on killing to succeed, we must kill."

"Today I call upon people around the world to bring an end to this madness and create a world economy based instead, on peace. Cease the development of unbounded horrendous methods of destruction. Demand your governments withdraw their fighting machines from other lands and use them only for defense. Stop the proliferation of weapons. If we don't finance our nations by selling death, the ability of mad men around the globe to use those weapons for offensive reasons will diminish drastically."

"I would like the germ of a new world economy to begin right here, this very night. All of you here and those of you listening, demand your leaders end the lavishing of our national treasures on weapons makers. Demand that this country, the strongest nation on earth, develop an economy of peace. I want each of you to begin, today, to create Profit Through Peace. I'm asking for neither a welfare state nor a national give away. I'm asking that you to demand of your government that our riches be used to develop a new and better home for all of us. Create new jobs for those who are now producing death, develop resources that enhance life and improve our world. Demand that our elected representatives reassign our taxes from death to life. We have more systems of destruction than we will ever possibly need to defend our borders. We need no more. Neither our souls nor our earth can sustain this economy based on hate."

"When we show the world that we can profit through peaceful measures, when we stop selling the means for countries to destroy one another, we will become the nation the entire globe will follow. When we export peace, we will create the planet our Spirit has asked of us."

"Which of you will take steps necessary to stop this madness?" The auditorium erupted.

"Who will follow the path demanded of us?" Everyone was on their feet. Television cameras panned the floor. I glanced to the wings and saw Kathryn, crying. I knew it was probably my final speech, my last chance to move the world before I was discredited or worse.

I pointed to a man in the front row that was now forced against the stage by the undulating crowd. I reached to him, took his hand and pulled him up with me. I held my arms in the air and within minutes the uproar faded to a mild din.

"Your name?" I asked. He looked at me, eyes wide with excitement. "Tell these people your name."

He looked at the crowd and said something. "The microphone," I tapped it "Speak into the Microphone."

He smiled at me and leaned into it, "Tim Lake," he said and held a hand in the air. Applause filled the room.

"Timothy," I asked, "Do you agree with what I've just said?"

He looked around as cheers and applause began to ring. He turned to me with a smile and nodded his head.

"Say it Timothy, Say it to the people. Say it so everyone, across the planet can hear you."

He turned to the microphone and as the noise grew, he shouted into the mike, "Yes! Yes I agree!"

"Tim, are you willing to become the catalyst for Profit Through Peace?"

He looked hesitant but when the crowd began to chant, "Profit Through Peace, Profit Through Peace," over and over. He was caught up in the enthusiasm. He leaned into the microphone and shouted, "Yes! Profit Through Peace!"

Pandemonium broke out. A camera was nearly in his face and he beamed at the attention. I put my hand on his shoulder. I knew what the coming weeks would bring and I felt guilty for what I had thrust upon him. I took his hand and raised it into the air, "I want to introduce the man who will save our country, the world, the earth itself, Timothy Lake."

Kathryn came from the wings and shouted into my ear, I couldn't hear her above the commotion. She took my arm and pulled me away. I couldn't leave the auditorium in chaos with this poor man at the heart of it. I raised my hands and the noise faded to a soft roar. "Listen, this is a huge job. If we intend to refocus the direction of our very government, it can't be done by one person. I want each and every one of you to help this man. I would like those of you who have the background, the ability and the courage to join Mr. Lake here on stage. We will have someone take your information and a team will come together."

People began crowding the stairs. Center security met the volunteers at the stairways to prevent them from coming on stage. From the wings came people with pads of paper and ink pens. They began to take information.

I looked at a TV cameras, "You who are watching, who want to change our world, want to follow the true direction, join us. Send your information to the Hult Center in Eugene, Oregon. Contact us by e-mail or letter and help this man. We can make this happen. We *are* God's hands."

Kathryn pulled harder and I yielded. She shouted into my ear but the auditorium was again chanting 'Profit Through Peace'. I heard nothing else as I left the stage. Cameras surrounded Mr. Lake and panned the bedlam from the floor. I don't believe anyone even noticed I was gone.

Behind the stage the din still echoed and I could finally hear what Kathryn was trying to say, "...could you do this? You knew they didn't want you to go there. And you jumped in with both feet. Jeremy, for God's sake, it's not just you, they'll destroy all of us because of this."

She led me to the elevator and when the door opened, Phillip was standing there. "They've brought everything from the hotel." He was panicked, "Annette is in the helicopter. Jeff is warming it up. We have to go. Now!"

Kathryn pulled me into the elevator and Phillip punched the button three times. As the door closed, the din from auditorium was cut to silence. We began to rise and Kathryn asked, "What's the evaluation? Can we fix this? Did he offer anything?"

Phillip looked at me then the floor, "Hunter said virtually nothing. It's impossible to read him. We're going to fly to Boise for some God forsaken reason, there we catch a military flight to DC for damage assessment. Everything else is canceled until they figure out where we go from here. Kathryn, I'm worried."

Phillip looked at me, he was terrified. We rode the elevator to the roof. The only sounds above the elevator's whine were our heavy breathing.

FORTY THREE

We stepped through the door into the helicopter and sat in silence. We four were the only passengers. The infamous 'Hunter' was nowhere to be seen. Just before the door began to close, a news team appeared from nowhere,

Lights and a camera lens were thrust through the opening. A reporter pushed his arm in and began to broadcast, "This is Randy Talmage, News Five at five, reporting from atop the Hult Center. I'm here with Jeremy Clay who is about to fly into the future after creating quite a stir here this evening.

"Mr. Clay, would you like to comment about your Profit Through Peace concept? How long have you planned this? Was Timothy Lake pre-selected to lead this movement? What brought you to choose him?"

Kathryn said, "No comment at this time. Please. We're a bit behind schedule. We have to go, I'm sorry."

Phillip gently moved the man's arm out and pulled the door closed.

"This was a very short presentation, Mr. Clay," the reporter shouted through the glass, "If you can wait a few short moments, our news bird would like to accompany you. Just a few moments..."

"Go, now!" A voice came from the front and the engines began to rev. The film team ducked low but lights still poured through the window. The cameraman held his equipment above his head as he crouched and the camera followed the window as the helicopter lifted into the air.

When we were fifty feet up the door to the rest room opened and out stepped a man I could only assume was Hunter. He leaned into the cockpit and spoke to Lehland then came back and sat in the shadows next to Phillip.

"It looks as though you've created quite a stir, Mr. Clay. Your impudence has already caused substantial damage. We'll have to determine if it's feasible to appease our associates or discontinue this charade. But," He turned to Kathryn, "Even if we can resolve the problems, should we? You, Mr. Clay, seem to have little respect for those who sustain you. Financially, you've upset quite a few of your benefactors. It may be difficult to regain their trust. "

"Trust? Who are you to talk about trust?" my voice echoed above the vibration of the engines.

Kathryn grabbed my arm, "Jeremy, I swear I didn't know about Ellen." She looked at Hunter, "Did you have anything to do with this? You promised you would just give her incentive to stay out of our hair."

Hunter laughed, "So this is all about that crazy woman in Ann Arbor, the blackmailer? You both know she had problems. She was bound to blow up at some point. Just an unfortunate incident. We didn't have to help her, after all she was facing ten years in prison."

I glared at him through the darkness, "Don't give me that shit, I know you had her killed."

"Don't be ridiculous. We spoke to her, tried to reason and then threatened her. Whatever happened after that was simply an unfortunate result of her bad judgment."

I stood up and held a grab bar. "You lying bastard, you had her murdered, don't try to tell me you didn't. Who's next, the guy in Eugene? Me? These people? You can't kill everyone you son of a bitch." I moved toward him.

Hunter shouted, "Clay, sit down!" he turned to Kathryn, "You said you could handle him, dammit, handle him before I get angry." He reached into his coat.

I froze and turned toward her. She looked as though she were pleading to me in the dim light. "So everything you did was to 'handle me'? To manipulate me and keep me where this asshole wanted me. To satisfy his associates?"

"Jeremy! It wasn't that. I truly...I..." She stammered.

"Enough of this shit. Jeremy, you're a pawn. A once in a lifetime opportunity to influence many, many things around this world. Your dear friends here were to direct the situation, to keep you on track. My God, I don't believe you actually consider yourself some sort of Deity?" He laughed out loud.

I jumped toward him. Phillip grabbed me and we fell to the floor with a huge thud. Lehland turned on the overhead lights, "Everyone OK back there?"

As I looked into the eyes of the man seated before me, my reoccurring nightmare returned. The eyes were of the man with the coat. He was no longer a phantom from my memory, he was front of me, with a gun pointed my way, again. "Everyone just relax. Get back to your seats."

"Is everything OK back there?" Lehland repeated.

"We're fine. Just a misunderstanding. How about you turn the lights back off. Everything's good back here."

He waved the gun at me, "Sit down Mr. Clay. Let's keep this civil. We might possibly redeem this disaster if you'll just take a deep breath and relax. We've got a long way to go and we'll be spending quite a bit of time together, so it's best if we agree to cooperate and put our issues aside for the moment."

We flew in silence for several minutes as the valley rose to mountains below us. The lights of towns disappeared and we were surrounded by a darkened emptiness.

Finally Hunter spoke, "Jeremy, we're not the enemy. We want what you want. We just want the changes to come at a pace that can be dealt with, to protect the economy, keep financial systems flowing. You've advocated an abrupt shut down to a major portion of this country's income. We just need to act with prudence, make changes without creating a depression. Can you begin to imagine what effects your suggestions could have? How many people might end up out of work and starving? You don't want people dying in the streets. And besides, this country could lose its superiority without our defense contractors. Do you want to be responsible for America becoming a second rate joke?"

I lost the feigned composure forced by his gun, "If you're so damned concerned and honorable, explain to me what happened at the rally in Washington?"

He spoke from the shadow in a sullen voice, "A mad man killed several people. You should know, you were in the middle of it."

My voice was harsh and low, "Senator Evans was the target,

wasn't he? Klein was hired to kill him to stop he investigation of these 'associates' you work for."

"Jeremy, I think you've been under too much stress. Believe me when I say we will get you the help you need. Kathryn assured us you could deal with all of this, but I think it's time you took a short break to get back on track."

I continued, "Your people hired Klein to assassinate Evans and kill everyone else involved with the investigations. He missed me somehow. There was still someone who could draw focus on the issues."

"Yes, it seems you're becoming delusional. Jeremy, Klein was crazy, his letters proved that. It was the very troops and the weapons you so disdain that stopped him, stopped him before he could finish you too. Let's keep this all in the proper context."

"I saw you, Hunter. I watched as they cut Klein to pieces. He was probably assured he'd be spared but I was still standing when he fell. I saw your face. It would have been only a matter of time before you were tied to all of it, the assassination, The Cape. I watched you aim at me and pull the trigger."

"Mr. Clay. Your error tonight could have been resolved. We may still be able to regain our position, however, these assertions you've imagined could make it extremely difficult for us to recover should they become public. I need assurance, this very moment, from you and your friends here that what you've just implied will go no further."

He looked through the dim light to each person in the helicopter, then faced me and raised his gun, "It's imperative that this story stops here Mr. Clay, for the sake of everyone involved."

I jumped from my seat and lunged forward while Phillip pushed the gun toward the roof. It went off with a sharp echo as I landed hard on Hunter's chest. Phillip grappled for the gun when Annette and Kathryn joined in subduing the man.

Lehland screamed from the cockpit, "What the hell's going on back there?" The Helicopter wavered in the air. A petroleum smell began to permeate the cabin.

The gun bounced to the floor as we wrestled with the man. He knew how to handle the situation and Kathryn was slammed against the wall opposite us. With a free hand he fisted Annette in the ear, knocking her to the floor.

Lehland yelled from the front, "Something's wrong, we're losing stability, I'm going to have to bring her down. Hold on."

Phillip searched the floor for the gun leaving me to struggle with Hunter. Kathryn stood and jumped toward us when the helicopter lurched again. I found myself on the floor next to

Phillip. Hunter lay beside me with Kathryn on top of him. As the helicopter settled further, there were loud snaps from tree limbs and the machine twisted sideways. We all ended in a pile across from the door. Annette lay motionless on the bottom.

I tried to grab Hunter around the shoulders and found my arm around his neck. I pulled hard. The copter hit something again and leaned the other way. As we slid toward the door I heard the engines rev until they sounded like they might explode.

The tail of the machine spun around and the helicopter righted itself just before coming to an awkward rest on the forest floor.

I looked up, saw the hatch handle and pulled it. The door sprung open. Hunter screamed, "Everybody stop. This goes no further." He rose to his knees with his back to the cockpit. He'd recovered the gun and aimed it at my chest. Phillip lay face down in shock, Annette was still unconscious and Kathryn sat on the floor beside Hunter, her back to the seats. The engines coughed and vibrated heavily and the smell of fuel was overwhelming.

Lehland rushed to the cabin and discovered the situation. He stopped and quietly backed away when he saw the gun.

"I'm afraid we have a serious problem with only a single resolution." He showed the same passionless determination he'd displayed months before as I watched him from the stage in DC. He lifted the gun to my face. I could almost see his joy as he took a breath. I closed my eyes. There was a dull thud accompanied by a sharp retort. I cringed but felt nothing.

Kathryn screamed, "Jump, Jeremy, now!"

I looked to see Hunter shaking his head, she had kicked him hard in the jaw. Phillip was up and grabbed at him again. I rolled out the door and landed on the soft forest floor.

Screaming came from the cabin and the engines began to rev. Once more the machine actually started to lift and wobble into the air.

I yelled to Kathryn, "Jump! Get out. Jump!" but moments later it was too late. The helicopter rose unsteady through the trees, flailing back and forth, sending a cascade of needles and branches down on me.

They made it past the tree tops and it looked as though they were flying safely when the engine stuttered and quit. The forest went silent for a split moment but was suddenly torn with the sound of rushing air, snapping limbs and the crush of metal. The night lit up with an explosion of flames.

I fell to the ground and lay my face on the cold earthy forest floor and sobbed.

From the darkness came the sound of rotors beating the air. I looked up to see a news copter approaching the crash site. Lights lit the sky and they circled as close as they safely could. I closed my eyes and hid in the darkness.

FORTY FOUR

I lay in the fir needles until the dawn brought a pale glow to the tree tops. Cold and exhausted, I began to make my way toward the crash to look for Kathryn. I struggled through the underbrush but after a several minutes, there were more aircraft nearing the site. Burned remains of the helicopter were strong on the wind and muted voices echoed through the trees.

Terrified that it might be Hunter's people, I turned back and made my way down the mountain. I trudged through the forest for nearly two hours when I came upon a river. The water was crystal and ice cold. I was hungry and thirsty and sipped from the stream until my body began to shudder from the chill.

I followed the river downward, climbing over outcrops of rock and around huge trees that grew from the bank. Early morning I came upon a gravel parking area at the head of a trail. I followed the road that led away from it to some pavement a mile or so further down the mountain.

After hiding from a few cars I waved down an old pickup with a driver who looked as though he'd just driven out of the 1970s. He smiled and nodded when I opened the door. I knew he could never be from the government. He wore a long ponytail and a full beard that must have been eight inches in length. He couldn't have been more than thirty years old. He never asked why I was out in the middle of nowhere dressed the way I was and I didn't offer an explanation.

We passed a road sign stating, "Detroit, 6 miles" and he pointed.

"Ours is a tad smaller than that other one. A bit more pleasant, I think." He smiled. I wondered if he recognized me or knew where I was from but he gave no indication he even cared.

We drove in silence for quite some time until he said, "I'll be turnin' off the highway up here a ways. Don't want to leave you in the middle of nowhere so if you'd like, I can drop you near the old lake resort. It'll be easier to catch a ride from there but if you want to stay a bit, its late season there should be a cabin or two available. It'll closes up for the winter. Betty's still open for hunters now and *she* stays year round. She might be pleased with some company if you decide to spend time."

He dropped me across from an old weather worn sign that read 'Detroit Lake Resort, ¾ mile, Open May thru October'.

I thanked him for the ride and started up a side road as he drove off leaving a trail of smoke behind.

After a short hike I arrived at the resort, although the place somewhat stretched the meaning of the word. It consisted of several old, one room cabins along the shore of the lake. Across a gravel lot, another was adorned with a sign that read 'OFFICE' in bold yellow letters. The office was slightly larger than the other cabins. I entered a room with a refrigerator unit, shelves filled with canned goods and an old worn desk scattered with papers. A pen in a holder stuck out of the mess at the front and beside that was a silver bell. A sign taped to the front of the desk read 'ING FOR SERVICE' The upper corner torn away but held with yellowing tape.

I tapped the bell and a voice came from somewhere, "Just a minute. Be right with you."

An elderly woman with thick glasses and a flowered dress came through a door. She stopped when she saw me and looked out the window. "Sorry, didn't hear you drive up." She looked concerned as she examined my wrinkled, filthy suit.

I smiled as much as I could, "A friend of yours dropped me off on the highway. Ponytail, long beard," I measured from my chin with my hands. "You must be Betty? He told me you might have a room available for a couple days. I've got cash. I really need to clean up and get some rest."

"Old Blue truck?" I nodded. "That's Robby He's a great boy, looks out for me up here." She opened the lap drawer, took out an old book and shuffled to an empty page.

It was as though I'd traveled back in time, No phones, no computers. She turned the book toward me and handed me the pen from the holder. I filled out the information and double checked so I might remember what I'd created. She turned the book back so she could study it and reached to a board of keys on the wall behind her.

"Here you are Mr. Lennon; you'll be in number three. There's a note on the table that tells about check out and such. You can get fishing poles and bait here and there's a rowboat, but you have to reserve it. Though that won't be a problem this time of year."

She looked me over again, "Gets pretty cold up here at night. There's a lost and found box in back. You might find some warm clothes in it."

I found some musty old clothing that would be much warmer than my suit. I gathered an arm load, bought some canned goods, a six pack of beer and paid cash.

At the cabin, I locked myself in, fell on the bed and passed out.

FORTY FIVE

'Three days now I've hidden in this room. Betty loaned me her newspapers on condition I return them when I'm done. She can't see well enough to read any more. She told me, "I keep getting both papers so I have something to start my fires in the winter, and besides, Old Dale Williams makes his living delivering and he needs the money".

I've kept the articles about my demise in the flaming helicopter. The bodies were burned beyond recognition. I've been haunted every waking moment and when I'm able to sleep the horror pervades my dreams as well.

Apparently Timothy Lake has gathered quite a following and is attempting to carry on my wishes. I pity what he'll have to deal with as it all goes forward but maybe he'll do better than I did.

I still don't know where I'll end up, what I'll do. I certainly don't want to be what they said I was. Hunter was right about that, I was beginning to believe the lies myself. Between bouts of depression over Kathryn and the loneliness that overwhelms me, it's been a wonder I haven't just ended it all.

As I stand here and breathe this thick fog I find it hard to even remember all that's happened this past six months. All my friends are gone. So much death. And through it all, I'm still here. Why? Why me?

People throughout the world swear they saw me, watched me perform miracles and save lives, in several countries at nearly the same time. How could that many people imagine these things? Could Hunter somehow have orchestrated it? Could someone else? Even so, why would they? Why the hell would they?

All in all it's been two months since the rally in Washington and my extended fifteen minutes of fame has begun to fade. Since I'm gone, incinerated on live TV, I should be able to move on soon. Maybe I'll grow a ponytail and an eight inch beard. I'll need a new alias. My current one, John Lennon, might raise a few eyebrows elsewhere..

It's cold in these mountains. I'd like to be someplace warm. San Diego would be an easy place to blend in. I could disappear there and start all over. Landscape would be a year round position.

A faint glow began to show above the mountains and brightened the fog. It was time to return to the solitude of my cabin. My feet were hidden by the mists that became frost on the dock. I eased along the boards and shuffled toward the shore.

The closer I came the more uneasy I felt. A whisper filtered through the darkness so I stopped and held my breath. Another voice responded. They both grew louder as they approached and I desperately searched for an escape. Everything, the dock, the lake and the shore were still shrouded in fog but I wasn't quite to the shore.

Several feet away a silhouette appeared in the mist and beside it a smaller one, a child.

My breath billowed in a huge cloud as I stepped off the dock into an inch or so of water and tried to avoid the people. I hoped to slink away before they saw me. I glided along the edge of the lake, next to the shore as rapidly as I could toward my cabin.

The two approached through a veil of white and their faces came into view.

I stopped without a word, cut off from my escape, and waited for them to continue.

"My God!" she said aloud to her son. "It's him."

She began to shout, "It's him! Go get your father, Hurry." As the pitch of her words increased, a man's voice ushered from the mist. "Linda? You OK?"

"Steve, come quick, it's Jeremy Clay, it's Him."

She shouted to no one, "My Dear God, He's returned. Jeremy

Clay has returned." She ran to me and fell to her knees on the wet shore.

Doors opened and more footsteps came toward me through the gravel. The boy pulled his father by the hand, shouting, "We saw him, he came across the water. He was walking on the lake. "

People appeared from nowhere. Within what seemed only minutes, cars began to arrive. I tried to move but I was surrounded. Several knelt in front of me in prayer. The sun rose higher and the mists glowed with a bright golden hue. More than twenty faces stared at me in awe. Cameras flashed through the fog.

I reached out and placed my hand on the woman's head.

Libstaff lives and writes at the beach

on Puget Sound in Washington State

He and his wife spend much of their

summer at their retreat known as

"The Muse"

www.ingramcontent.com/pod-product-compliance
Lightning Source LLC
Chambersburg PA
CBHW060400260626
47160CB00006B/2385